BLOOMFIELD TOWNSHIP PUBLIC LIBRARY

3 1160 00522 2505

D1172435

BLOOMFIELD TOWNSHIP PUBLIC LIBRARY
1099 Lone Pine Road
Bloomfield Hills, Michigan 48302-2410

The Last Woman in His Life

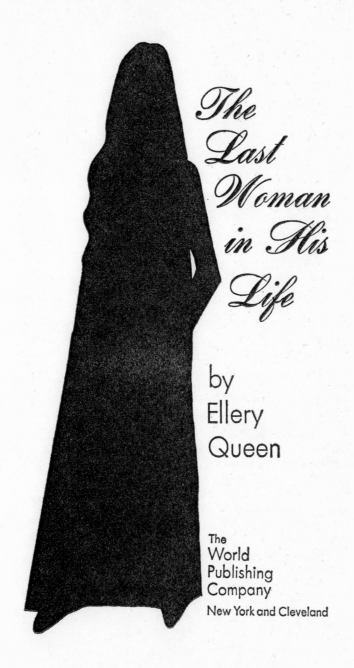

The Last Woman in His Life

by
Ellery
Queen

The
World
Publishing
Company
New York and Cleveland

BLOOMFIELD TOWNSHIP PUBLIC LIBRARY
1099 Lone Pine Road
Bloomfield Hills, Michigan 48302-2410

Copyright © 1969 by Ellery
Queen

All rights reserved. No part of
this book may be reproduced in
any form without written
permission from the publisher,
except for brief passages included
in a review appearing in a
newspaper or magazine.

Printed in the United States of
America

Contents

APR 1 9 2003

1.
The
First
Life

And so Ellery stood there, watching the BOAC jet take the Scot away.

He was still standing alone on his island when a hand touched his.

He turned around and it was, of all people, Inspector Queen.

"El," his father said, squeezing his arm. "Come on, I'll buy you a cup of coffee."

The old boy always comes through, Ellery thought over his second cup in the airport restaurant.

"Son, you can't monkey around in this business without once in a while running into the back of your own hand," the Inspector said. "It didn't have to happen this way. You let yourself get involved with the guy. If I allowed myself that kind of foolishness I'd have had to toss my shield in years ago. Human flesh can't stand it."

Ellery raised his hand as if the other were on the Bible. "So help me Hannah, I'll never make that mistake again."

Having said this, he found his glance coming to rest

on Benedict and Marsh, in man-to-man conversation
at the other side of the dining room.

All men, Shaw said, mean well.

Not excluding Ellery. What was this but the familiar
Chance Encounter? Time lines converging for the moment, a brief nostalgia, then everyone on his way and
no harm done?

Had he but known.

It began, as such apparently meaningless reunions
do, with grips, grins, and manly warmth. The pair immediately accepted Ellery's invitation to move over
to the Queen table. They had not laid eyes on him, and
vice versa, since Harvard.

To Inspector Queen, Marsh was just a citizen named
Marsh. But he had certainly heard of Benedict—
Johnny-B to the world of jet, a charter member of
Raffles, fixed star of the lady columnists, crony of nobil-
ity, habitué of Monaco, Kitzbühel, and the yachting
isles of Greece. January might find Benedict at the
winter festival in Málaga; February in Garmisch-
Partenkirchen; March in Bloemfontein for the national
games; April at the Songkran Festival in Chiangmai;
May in Copenhagen for the royal ballet; June at Epsom
Downs for the English Oaks and at Newport and Cork
for the transatlantic yacht races; July at Henley and
Bayreuth; August at Mystic for the Outdoor Art Festival; September in Luxembourg for the wine; October
in Turin for the auto show; November at Madison
Square Garden for the horse show; and December at
Makaha Beach for the surfing championships. These
were only typical; Johnny-B had a hundred other enter-
tainments up his sleeve. Ellery had always thought of
him as a run-for-your-life man without the pathologi-
cal stop-watch.

John Levering Benedict III toiled not (toil, he liked
to argue, was man's silliest waster of time), neither did
he spin except in the social whirl. He was charming

without the obvious streak of rot that ran through his
set, a fact that never palled on the press assigned to the
Beautiful People. He was even handsome, a not common attribute of his class (in whom the vintage tended
to sour)—on the slight side, below-average tall, with
fine fair hair women adored stroking, and delicate
hands and feet. He was, of course, sartorially ideal;
year after year he sauntered onto the Ten Best-Dressed
list. There was something anciently Grecian about him,
a to-the-bone beauty as fine as the texture of his hair.

Johnny-B's paternal grandfather had staked out a
stout chunk of the Olympic Peninsula and the timber-
lands around Lake Chelan to become one of the earliest
lumber barons of the Pacific Northwest. His father had
invested in shipping, piling Pelion on Ossa—that is to
say, according to the gossip, leaving the difficulty of
spending the resultant riches to Johnny. In Johnny's
set it was often pointed out that with a fortune in the
multimillions the feat could not easily be done; that
past a certain point great wealth is hard to redistribute.
That Johnny tried manfully is a matter of public record.
Alimony apparently made mere dents, only enough to
bruise; he had just divorced his third wife.

The leash on the runaway tendencies of Johnny Benedict was said to be Al Marsh. Marsh, too, came from
a society tree, and he was luxuriously nested in his
own right from birth. But he grew up to toil and spin,
from choice. With Marsh it was not a question of ava-
rice or anxiety over his wealth; he worked, said those
who knew him well, because the life-style of his world
bored him. Dilettantism *in vacuo* had no appeal for
him. He had taken top honors at Harvard Law, gone
on to serve a brilliant apprenticeship to a United States
Supreme Court justice, and emerged into the cynical
realities of Washington and New York to found a law
firm of his own that, with the aid of his family's influence and connections, quietly acquired a sterling clien-

tele and a hallmark reputation. He had offices in both
cities.

Experts in such matters nominated Marsh one of the
matrimonial catches of any season whatever. He was
unfailingly attractive to women, whom he handled with
the same tact he brought to his practice of law, and not
only because he was elusive. He was a bigger man
than Benedict, darkly rugged, with a smashed nose
from his college wrestling days, a jaw that looked as
if it had been mined in Colorado, and a naturally
squinty set to the eyes—"the Marlboro type," Johnny
called him affectionately—who seemed born to saddle
horses and foreign cars. He had a fondness for both
which he indulged when he could find the time, and a
passion for flying; he piloted his own plane with a grim
devotion that could only be explained by the fact that
his father had died in one.

As so often happens in the case of men to whom
women respond, other men did not take to Marsh easily. Some called it his aloofness, others his reserve,
others his "standoffishness"; whatever it was, it caused
Marsh to have a very small circle of friends. Johnny
Benedict was one of the few.

Their relationship was not altogether personal.
Johnny had inherited from his father the services of
an ancient and prestigious law firm which had handled
three generations of Benedict investments; but for the
management of his personal affairs he relied on Marsh.

"Of course you just flew in from the moon," Ellery
said. "It's about the only place, from what I hear,
you've never been."

"Matter of fact, I got off the jet from London fifteen
minutes ago, and Al here got off with me," Benedict
said. "We had some business in London, and th-then
there was that auction at S-Sotheby's."

"Which of course you had to attend."

"Please," Marsh said in a pained way. "Amend the

auxiliary verb. I know of no law that compels a man to drop what Johnny just dropped for that Monet."

Benedict laughed. "Aren't you always lecturing me about spending my m-money so I've a fighting chance for a profit?" He not only stammered, he had difficulty with his r's, giving his speech a definite charm. It was hard to see a rapacious capitalist in a man who pronounced it "pwofit."

"Are you the guy who bought that thing?" Inspector Queen exclaimed. "Paid all that loot for a hunk of old canvas and a few francs' worth of paint?"

"Don't tell us what you got it for, Johnny," Ellery said. "I can't retain figures like that. I suppose you're going to convert it into a dartboard for your game room, or something equally kicky?"

Marsh signaled for the waiter. "You've been listening to Johnny's detractors. Another round, please. He really knows art."

"I really do," Benedict said, pronouncing it "weally." "So help m-me Ripley. I'd like you to see my c-collection sometime." He added politely, "You, too, Inspector Queen."

"Thanks, but include me out," the Inspector said. "My son calls me a cultural barbarian. Behind my back, of course. He's too well brought up to say it frontwards."

"As for me, Johnny," Ellery said, scowling at pater, "I don't believe I could bear it. I've never quite adjusted to the unequal distribution of wealth."

"How about the unequal distribution of brains?" Benedict retorted. "From what I've read about you and the Glory Guild case, not to m-mention all those other mental miracles you bring off, you're a second cousin of Einstein's." Something in Ellery's face drove the banter from Benedict's voice. "Have I said s-something?"

"Ellery's fagged," his father said quickly. "The Guild case was a tough one, and just before that he'd been on a round-the-world research trip in some far-out places where there's no charge for the bedbugs or trots, and *that* took the starch out of his hide. As a matter of fact, I've some vacation time coming, and we were thinking of taking off for a couple of weeks of peace and quiet somewhere."

"Ask Johnny," Marsh said. "He knows all the places, especially the ones that aren't listed."

"No, thanks," Ellery said. "Not Johnny's places."

"You've got the w'ong idea about me, Ellery," Benedict protested. "What's today?"

"Monday."

"No, the date."

"March twenty-third."

"Well, just before I flew to London—on the nineteenth, if you want to check—I was in Valencia for the Festival of St. Joseph. W-wild? Before that I attended the Vienna Spring Fair, and before *that*—the third, I think—I was in Tokyo for the dollie festival. How's that? C-cultural, wouldn't you say? Non-wastrel? Al, am I bragging again?"

"Brag on, Johnny," Marsh said. "That kind of self-puff helps your image. God knows it can use help."

Ellery remarked, "Dad and I were thinking of something less, ah, elaborate."

"Fresh air, long walks, fishing," Inspector Queen said. "Ever go fishing, Mr. Benedict? I mean in a mountain stream all by your lone, with a rod that didn't cost three hundred dollars? The simple pleasures of the poor, that's what we're after."

"Then you may call me Doc, Inspector, because I have just the prescription for you both." Benedict glanced at Marsh. "Are you with it, Al?"

"Ahead of you," Marsh chuckled. "A rowboat gets you a cabin cruiser Ellery doesn't know."

"Know?" Ellery said. "Know what?"

"I own a place up in New England," Johnny Benedict said, "that very few people are aware I h-have.

Not a bit doggy, plenty of w-woods, an unpolluted stream stocked with you name it—and I've fished it with a spruce pole I cut and trimmed myself, Inspector, and had splendid luck—and a guest cottage about a quarter of a mile from the main h-house that's as private as one of d-dear Ari's deals. It's all terribly *heimisch*, Ellery, and I know you and your f-father would enjoy it. You're welcome to use the cottage for as long as you like. I give you my oath no one will bother you."

"Well," Ellery began, "I don't know what to say . . . ."

"I do," the Inspector said promptly. "Thank you!"

"I mean, where in New England?"

Benedict and Marsh exchanged amused glances again. "Smallish town," Benedict said. "Doubt if you've heard of it, Ellery. Of no c-consequence whatsoever. Wightsville."

"Wightsville?" Ellery stopped. *"Wrightsville?* You, Johnny? Own property up there?"

"For years and years."

"But I never knew!"

"Told you. I've kept it top-hush. Bought it through a dummy, just so I could have a place to let my hair d-down when I want to get away from it all, which is oftener than you'd think."

"I'm sorry, Johnny," Ellery said, beating his breast. "I've been an absolute stinker."

"It's modest—bourgeois, in fact. Down my great-grandfather's alley. He w-was a carpenter, by the way."

"But why Wrightsville, of all places?"

Benedict grinned. "You've advertised it enough."

"Well, I swan. Wrightsville happens to be my personal prescription for what periodically ails me."

"As if he didn't know," Marsh said. "He's followed your adventures, Ellery, the way Marcus Antonius followed Caesar's. Johnny's especially keen on your Wrightsville yarns. Keeps checking them for mistakes."

"This, gentlemen, is going to be the resumption of a beautiful friendship," Ellery said. "You sure we wouldn't be putting you out, Johnny?"

They went through the time-honored ritual of protest and reassurance, shook hands all around, and that evening a messenger brought an envelope that contained two keys and a scribbled note:

> "Dear Sour-Puss: The smaller key is to the guest house. The other unlocks the main house, in case you want to get in there for something—grub, booze, clothing, whatever, it's always stocked. (So is the guest house, by the way, though not so bountifully.) Use anything you need or want from either place. Nobody's up there now (I have no live-in caretaker, though an old character named Morris Hunker comes out from town occasionally to keep an eye on things), and judging from the foul mood you were in today you need all the healing solitude my retreat in Wrightsville can provide. *Bonne chance,* and don't grouch your old man—he looks as if he can use some peace, too.
>
>   Fondly,
>   Johnny
>
> P.S.: I may come up there soon myself. But I won't bother you. Not unless you want to be bothered."

The Queens set down at Wrightsville Airport a few minutes past noon the next day.

The trouble with Wrightsville—and Wrightsville had developed trouble, in Ellery's view—was that it had perfidiously kept step with the twentieth century.

Where his favorite small town was concerned Ellery was a mossback conservative, practically a reactionary. He was all for Thursday night band concerts in Memorial Park, with the peanut and popcorn whistles chirping tweet-tweet like excited birds, the streets lined with gawky boys ogling self-conscious girls and people from the outlying farms in town in their town-meetin' best;

and Saturday the marketing day, with the black-red mills of Low Village shut down and High Village commerce swinging.

He felt a special attachment for the Square (which was round), with its periphery of two-story frame buildings (except for the Hollis Hotel, which towered five stories, and Upham House, a three-and-attic Revolutionary-era inn); in its mathematical center the time-treated memorial to Jezreel Wright, who had founded Wrightsville on an abandoned Indian site in 1701—a bronze statue long since turned to verdigris and festooned with so many bird droppings it looked like a modern sculpture, and at its feet a trough which had watered half a dozen generations of Wrightsville horseflesh. The Square was like a wheel with five spokes leading from its hub: State Street, Lower Main, Washington, Lincoln, Upper Dade; the grandest of these being State with its honor guard of century-old trees, the repository of the gilt-domed red-brick Town Hall and the County Court House building (how many times had he walked up the alley to the side entrance that opened into the Wrightsville police department!), the Carnegie Library across the street (where it was still possible to find books by Henty, Richard Harding Davis, and Joseph Hergesheimer!), the Chamber of Commerce building, the Wrightsville Light & Power Company, and the Northern State Telephone Company; and far from least, at the State Street entrance to Memorial Park, the Our Boys Memorial and the American Legion bandstand. About the Square in those days had been displayed some of the finest fruit of Wrightsville's heritage—the tiny gold *John F. Wright, Pres.* on the dusty windows of the Wrightsville National Bank, the old Bluefield Store, the "Minikin Road" on the street marker visible from the corner window of the Bon Ton, and half a dozen other names passed down from the founding families.

Upper Whistling Avenue, which crossed State Street a block northeast of the Square, led up to Hill Drive, where some of the oldest residential properties had stood (even older ones, great square black-shuttered clapboard affairs, most gone to pot even in Ellery's earliest acquaintance, occupied the farther reaches of State Street). Upper Dade ran northwest up to North Hill Drive, which had been taken over by the estates of Wrightsville's *nouveaux riches* (a *nouveau riche*, in the view of the Wrights, Bluefields, Dades, Granjons, Minikins, Livingstons, *et al.*, being anyone who had made his pile after the administration of Rutherford B. Hayes).

Most of this was gone. The store fronts of the Square were like the façades of the commercial buildings fronting Ventura Boulevard in the San Fernando Valley running out of Hollywood, one of Ellery's favorite abominations—lofty modernisms in glass, stucco, redwood, and neon absurdly dwarfing the mean little stores that cowered behind them. The Hollis, which risked a new marquee just before World War II, had recklessly undertaken a complete face-lift, coming out contemporary and (to his mind) disgusting. The New York Department Store and the High Village Pharmacy had vanished, and the Bon Ton had taken over the entire plinth between Washington and Lincoln Streets and rebuilt from the ground up what to Ellery's sickened eye was a miniature Korvette's. The Atomic War Surplus Outlet Store was of course no more, and the eastern arc of the Square was almost all new.

On the high ground to the north, matters were even worse. Lovely old Hill Drive had fallen before the invading developers (a few houses had been saved, after a last-ditch battle by the Landmarks Commission of the Wrightsville Historical Society, as "historic sites"); the old Hill grandeur was today a solid rank of highrise apartment buildings, frowning down on the town below like concentration camp guards. Many of the extensive estates on North Hill Drive had been sold and the section rezoned for one-acre stands of middle-income private homes. Wrightsville's humbler suburbs mushroomed to beyond the airport, where whole new communities with regional monickers like New Village and Mahogany Acres had sprouted. At least thirty-five farms Ellery had known and cherished were extinct. There were new factories by the dozen, chiefly neat little plants by the wayside making electronic parts on subcontract to the giants working for the Department of Defense. Even Twin Hills and Sky Top Road, to which the well-to-do had inevitably fled, were beginning to grow tentacles.

And most of the old families had withered away, or the culls of their descendants had given up, hacked off their roots, and rerooted elsewhere.

Still, to Ellery it was Wrightsville. The cobbled streets of Low Village remained, the poor being America's last caretakers of old things. The Willow River that serviced the mills ran as yellow and red and turquoise as ever without noticeable effect on the immortal old willows and alders on its banks that sucked on its poisonous brew. Al Brown's Ice Cream Parlor and the refaced Wrightsville Record building on Lower Main off the Square stood their ground. And the surrounding hillsides still beamed benign, with the muscular Mahoganies beyond promising to withstand any onslaught of man except a saturation attack by hydrogen bombs, which was unlikely, Wrightsville being too unimportant (the town kept reassuring itself) in the scheme of things.

So, to Ellery's eye, Wrightsville with all its flaws was a still-viable Shangri-la.

He hired a Cougar at the car-rental agency in the airport and the Queens, gladly gulping lungfuls of genuine air, drove out to Benedict's hideaway.

From the way Benedict had talked Ellery expected a dilettante twenty or thirty acres. They found instead a two-hundred-acre spread of timber, water, and uncut pasture halfway between Wrightsville and Shinn Corners, in a farmed-out section of the valley where it began to creep up into the northwestern hills. The property was barred off by tall steel fencing and posted against hunting, fishing, and trespassing generally, in large and threatening signs bolted to the fence.

"Used to be all dairy farms out this way," Ellery complained as he got out to open the main gate. "The sweetest herds you ever saw."

"Well, don't blame Benedict," his father said. "They were probably given up before he bought them out. Small farms are going out of business all over New England."

"Still," Ellery carped, and he got back into the car with a slam.

The dirt road took them past the main house, which was a few hundred yards in from the entrance, apparently one of the original farmhouses of the property, a spready old two-story clapboard, with half a dozen chimneys, that appeared to house twelve or fifteen rooms. A quarter of a mile farther in they came to the guest house, a five-room Cape Cod-type cottage with a recent look. It lay deep in the woods, in a glade that had been hacked out to let the sun through. As they got out of the Cougar they heard a brook that seemed to be in a hurry and was making a great deal of noise about it.

"Sounds as if we could cast a line right out the bedroom window," the Inspector said. "Man, what a way to live!"

"If somebody else bakes the bread," Ellery said sourly.

"Ellery, what in hell is the matter with you?" his father cried. "If you think I'm going to put up with a

prima donna for two weeks . . . ! We'd better have
this out right now. It was plain damn decent of your
friend to offer you this place. The least you can do if
you feel like bellyaching is keep it to yourself. Or so
help me I'll take the next plane back to New York!"

It was a long time since Inspector Queen had talked
to him that way, and it so astounded Ellery that he
backed off and shut up.

They found the inside of the cottage as *heimisch* as
Benedict had advertised. No Park Avenue decorator
had been at work here. The furniture—Ellery checked
the labels—came from A. A. Gilboon's in High Village,
and the household fixtures and hardware had been
purchased at Clint Fosdick's or Hunt & Keckley's, or
both. "Bon Ton" was written all over the rest. It was
a homely, cheerful little place that was long on chintz,
"peasant" ware, and rag rugs, and had a fireplace in
the living room that made his palms itch for the poker.
The shelves held books; there was a stereo and a collection of cartridge tapes; and, tucked away in a corner
as if to say there was no law requiring its use, a portable
color TV.

The Inspector volunteered to unpack and get them
settled while Ellery drove down into town to supple-
ment the larder. They had found plenty of steaks,
chops, and poultry in the freezer and a generous supply of canned goods, but they needed perishables—
milk, bread, butter, eggs, fresh fruit and vegetables.

"Pick up something, too, son," the Inspector said,
"at what's-his-name's, Dunc MacLean's. Rye, Scotch,
vodka, anything to warm the bones."

"Unnecessary." Ellery waved. "You missed that re-
tractable bar in the living room, dad. It's stocked with
everything from absinthe to zubrovka."

He passed up Logan's Market on Slocum between
Upper Whistling and Washington—he was known there
—in favor of the supermarket across the street, where

he might expect to go unnoticed. As it was, he had to avert his face to avoid two women he thought he recognized. The trip into town depressed him further; the changes were too numerous and, to his eye, all for the worse. He was glad to get back to the cottage, where he found his father in slacks and an open-neck shirt lolling before a fire with a glass of brown waters in his fist.

"Yes, siree," the Inspector said happily, "this is *the* life."

The old man gave Ellery his head. He neither pushed nor pulled, contenting himself with a suggestion here or there and saying nothing if Ellery begged off. On Wednesday the Inspector spent most of the day fishing (in spite of Benedict's boast about cutting his own spruce pole, the old man found a roomful of sporting equipment that included some superb rods) and hauled in a mess of gorgeous trout for their dinner. Ellery spent that day on his spine's end, listening to Mozart and Bach, with a fillip of Tijuana Brass, and occasionally snoozing off. That night he slept the night through without benefit of sleeping pill or a dream he could recall on awakening—his first unbroken sleep in weeks; he had been living on nightmares. On Thursday the Queens explored the property, tramping over most of Benedict's two hundred acres and coming back ravenous; they devoured a couple of prodigious steaks Ellery charcoal-broiled on the backyard barbecue along with some husky baked potatoes topped with his favorite sour cream and chives. The Inspector pretended not to notice that Ellery polished his plate—the old man had not seen him finish a dinner for weeks.

Ellery had just turned on the dishwasher when he was startled by a jarring buzz. It seemed to come from what looked like an intercom. He snatched the receiver and said, "Who the devil is this?"

"Johnny," Benedict's voice said. "How's the patient?"

"Johnny? I'm just beginning to unlax." Had Benedict followed him up? "Oh, I see, this thing is hooked up to the main house. Two-way?"

"Yes. Ellery, I know I promised not to b-bother you—"

"When did you get in?"

"Late this afternoon. Look, there's s-something I have to tell you. Is it all right if I walk down and palaver for a minute?"

"Don't be a horse's patoot."

Ellery hung up and went to the bedroom the Inspector was using. The old man was just getting into his pajamas.

"Dad, Benedict's here. Wants to talk to us. Or to me. He's coming over from the main house now. Do you want to sit in on this?"

They looked at each other.

"You sound mysterious," Inspector Queen said.

"I'm not looking for trouble, you and God believe you me," Ellery said. "But there's a smell about this."

"All right. But I hope you're wrong, son."

Ten minutes later Ellery admitted a preoccupied Johnny-B—preoccupied, and something more. Worried? Whatever it is, Ellery assured himself, I'm staying out of it with both feet.

"Come in, Johnny."

"Forgive the pajamas and robe, Mr. Benedict," the Inspector said. "I had a strenuous day pacing off your property. I was just going to bed."

"Drink, Johnny?"

"Not just now, thanks." Benedict sank into a chair and looked around. His smile was perfunctory. Something was wrong, all right. The Queens did not glance at each other. "Like it up here?"

"I want to thank you properly, Johnny. I'm really beholden. This is exactly what I needed."

"Ellery and me both," the Inspector said.

Benedict's fine hand fluttered. Here it comes, Ellery thought. "Ellery?"

"Yes, Johnny."

"What I want to tell you. I'm h-having guests this w-weekend."

"Oh?"

"No, no, I'm not booting you out! They'll all stay at the main house. Acres of room there. Al Marsh is due up tomorrow, and Al's secretary—girl named Susan Smith—is coming Saturday evening. Also due tomorrow—" Benedict hesitated, made a face, and shrugged "—my three exes."

"Ex-wives?"

"Ex-wives."

"Excuse me for gawking, Johnny. What is this, Homecoming Week?"

The Inspector decided to improve on the light note. "I've always read what an interesting life you lead, Mr. Benedict, but this is ridiculous!"

They all laughed, Benedict weakly. "I wish it were as funny as that. Well. The point is, I don't want you people to be in any way discombobulated. There's nothing social or nostalgic about this get-together. Strictly b-business, if you know w-what I mean."

"I don't, but that's all right, Johnny. You don't owe us an explanation."

"But I can't have you thinking I'm an Indian giver. You won't be disturbed, I give you my w-word."

It all seemed so unnecessary that Ellery had to fight down his curiosity. They were a long way from the Harvard Yard, and he realized suddenly that he knew very little about Johnny-B that mattered. He had thought the invitation genuine. But had Benedict had an ulterior purpose . . . ?

Having given his word, Benedict stopped talking. He seemed hung up on a problem. The silence became depressing.

"Something wrong, Johnny?" Ellery asked. And cursed himself for having opened the door.

"Does it sh-show that much? I think I'll take that drink now, Ellery. No, I'll make it myself." Benedict jumped up and activated the bar. It was of the rotating type, swiveling out of the wall. He poured himself a stiff Scotch on the rocks and when he came back he said abruptly, "I have a favor to ask of both of you. I hate asking favors, I don't know why . . . but this one I have to."

"We're under obligation to you, Mr. Benedict," the Inspector said, smiling, "not the other way around."

"There's hardly anything within reason we could refuse you, Johnny," Ellery said. "What's the problem?"

Benedict set his glass down. He pulled a long single sheet of white paper from his breast pocket. It was folded in three. He unfolded it.

"For the record, this is my last w-will and testament." He said this in an oddly chill tone; to Ellery's sensitized ears it sounded like a sentence in a capital crime. Benedict felt his pockets. "I've simply got to start carrying a pen," he said. "May I borrow yours, Ellery?" He stooped over the coffee table. "I'll sign this and date it, and I ask you b-both to w-witness. Will you?"

"Naturally."

"Of course, Mr. Benedict."

They noted how he concealed the holograph text with his forearm as he wrote. When he was finished he flapped the sheet over so that only the bottom lay exposed. He indicated where the Queens were to sign, and they did so. He returned Ellery's pen, produced a long envelope, folded the will, slipped it into the envelope, sealed it, hesitated, and suddenly offered it to Inspector Queen.

"Could I ask you to k-keep this for me, Inspector? For a short w-while?"

"Well . . . sure, Mr. Benedict."

"I don't blame you for looking kind of puzzled," Benedict said in a hearty way. "But there's no big deal about this. Marsh is going to draw up a formal will for me over the weekend—that's why his secretary is coming—but I wanted something down on paper in the meantime." He laughed; it seemed forced. "I'm getting to the age when life looks more and more uncertain. Here today and here tomorrow—m-maybe. Right?"

They laughed dutifully, and when Benedict finished his Scotch he said good night and left. He seemed relieved.

Ellery was not. He shut the front door carefully and said, "Dad, what do you make of all that?"

"A lot of question marks." The Inspector stared at the blank envelope in his hands. "With the money he's got—and lawyers like Marsh—it's a cinch he's had a formal will practically from birth. So this thing he wrote out in longhand that we just witnessed supersedes the previous one."

"Not merely supersedes it, dad," Ellery said. "Changes it, or why a new will at all? The question is, what does it change it from, and what does it change it to?"

"Neither of which is your business," his father pointed out.

"This obviously involves his ex-wives," Ellery murmured; he was back at his pacing, the Inspector noted uneasily. "Business weekend. . . . No, I don't care for the smell of this."

"I can see I'll have to put off that shuteye for a while." The Inspector went to the bar. "I think you can use one, son. What'll it be?"

"Nothing. No, thanks."

"Who are the lucky ladies?"

"What?"

"The women he married. Do you know?"

"Of course I know. The Benedict Saga's always fas-

cinated me. His first wife came out of a chorus line in
Vegas. A bosomy redhead named Marcia Kemp, a sex-
pot who was thick with some really rough characters
until Johnny plucked her out of the state and made an
honest woman of her."

"Marcia Kemp." The old man nodded. "I remember
now. That one lasted—how long was it? Three months?"

"Closer to four. Mrs. Benedict number two was
Audrey Weston, a blonde with acting ambitions who
didn't have the talent to make it on Broadway or in
Hollywood. She gets a small part now and then, mostly
in TV commercials. But Johnny evidently thought she
was Oscar or Emmy material—for five or six months,
anyway."

"And number three?" the Inspector asked, sipping
his Chivas.

"Number three," Ellery said, "I have particular reason to recall." He was still pacing. "Alice Tierney. The
reason I paid special attention to Alice Tierney is that
I'd read she came from Wrightsville. One of the columnists. Naturally that titillated me, although the name
Tierney was unfamiliar to me. Or maybe that's why.
Anyway, it seems that this Tierney girl—in her news
photos a rather plain-looking brunette—was a trained
nurse. Johnny ran his Maserati or whatever he was
driving then off a country road—it must have been
around Wrightsville somewhere, though the piece
didn't say—and was laid up for a long stretch at his
'country home,' the story said, which I realize now
must have been the main house here. If Wrightsville
ever came into the stories I missed it, which is unlikely;
my hunch is that Johnny paid one of his patented *quid
pro quos* to keep the Wrightsville hideaway here out
of the columns. At any rate, Nurse Tierney was hired
on a sleep-in basis to take care of her famous patient,
and enforced proximity to a female for several weeks,
even a plain one, was apparently more than Johnny

could resist. After the usual Benedict-type courtship
he married the Tierney girl. That lasted the longest—
nine and a half months. He was legally unhitched only
a month or so ago."

"A redheaded Vegas mob girl, a New York no-talent
blonde actress, a brunette plain-Jane small-town nurse,"
the Inspector mused. "Doesn't sound as if they have
much in common."

"They do, though. They're all huge women.
Amazons."

"Oh, one of those. The little guy who keeps shooting
for Mount Everest. Must give fellows like Benedict a
sense of power, like when they get behind the wheel
of a souped-up car."

"My innocent old man," Ellery said with a grin. "I'll
have to give you a couple of sex-and-psychiatry books
appropriately marked. . . . And he's asked all three up
for the weekend, along with his lawyer, for a change
of will—or at least he says so—and he's kind of nervous
about it all. You know something, dad?"

"What now?"

"I don't like it. One bit."

The Inspector brandished his glass. "And you know
what, sonny? You're going to quit this racing up and
down like that road runner in the commercials and
you're going to sit down here and watch the Thursday
night movie—*right now*—and this weekend you'll keep
your schnozz strictly out of your friend Benedict's affairs—*whatever* they are!"

Ellery did his best, which faltered only once. On
Friday evening after dinner he felt the healthful need
to walk. Making an instant diagnosis, the Inspector
said, "I'll join you." When they got outdoors Ellery
turned in the direction of the hunted like a yellow
hound dog. His father seized the quivering paw. "*This*
way," he said firmly. "We'll go listen to the music of

the brook." "Poetry really doesn't become you, dad. If I'd wanted to communicate with Euterpe I'd have used the stereo." "Ellery, you're not going down to that house!" "Now come on, dad. I'm not going to barge in on them or anything like that." "Damn it all to hell!" shouted the old man, and he stamped back into the cottage.

When Ellery got back his father said anxiously, "Well?"

"Well what, dad?"

"What's going on down there?"

"I thought you weren't interested."

"I didn't say I wasn't interested. I said we oughtn't to get involved."

"House is lit up like Times Square. No sounds of girlish laughter, however. It can't be much of a party."

The Inspector grunted. "At least you had the sense to turn around and come back."

But they were not to remain uninvolved. A few minutes past noon on Saturday—the old man was about to lie down for a nap—there was a knock on the door and Ellery opened it to a very tall blonde girl with the bony structure and empty face of a fashion model.

"I'm Mrs. Johnny Benedict the Two," she said in a drawl that sounded Method-Southern to Ellery's ears.

"Of course. You're Audrey Weston," Ellery said.

"That's my professional name. May I come in?"

Ellery glanced at his father and stood aside. The Inspector came forward quickly. "I'm Richard Queen," he said. He had always had an eye for pretty girls, and this one was prettier than most, although in a blank sort of way. Her face looked as if it had been stamped out of a mold, like a doll's.

"Inspector Queen, isn't it? Johnny's told us you two were staying at the guest cottage—practically threatened to knock our heads together if we didn't leave you alone. So, of course, here I am." She turned her gray, almost colorless, eyes on Ellery. "Aren't you going to offer me a drink, dahling?"

She used her eyes and hands a great deal. Someone had evidently told her that she was the Tallulah Bankhead type, and she had never got over it.

Ellery gave her a Jack Daniels and a chair, and she leaned back with her long legs crossed and a long cigaret smoldering in the long fingers with the long fingernails that held the glass. She was dressed in a floppy silk blouse in fashionably wild colors and a calfskin skirt that was more mini than most, to her cost, for it revealed shanks rather than thighs. A matching leather jacket was draped over her shoulders. "And aren't you wondering why I disobeyed Johnny?" she drawled.

"I was sure you'd get around to it, Miss Weston," Ellery said, smiling. "I ought to tell you right off that I'm here with my father at Johnny's kind invitation to get away from problems. This is a problem, isn't it?"

"If it is—" the Inspector began.

"My evening gown is missing," Audrey Weston said.

"Missing?" the Inspector said. "A dress?"

"What do you mean missing?" Ellery said, leaning into the wind. "Mislaid?"

"Gone."

"Stolen?"

"You want to hear about it, dahling?"

"Oh. Well. As long as you're here. . . ."

"That gown set me back a bundle. It's all black sequins, an Ohrbach copy of a Givenchy original, with an absolutely illegal back and a V-front open to the bel—navel. And man, I want it back! Sure it was stolen. You don't just mislay a gown like that. At least I don't."

Her speech had been accompanied by so many vehement gestures and poses that Ellery felt tired for her.

"It probably has the simplest explanation, Miss Weston. When did you see it last?"

"I wore it to dinner last night—Johnny likes formality with women around, and when in Rome, y'know. . . . Even if the Roman is your ex."

So she expected to get something out of Johnny-B this weekend. Probably all three of them . . . Ellery tucked the surmise away. As if he were on the case. Case? Which case? There was no case. Or was there?

"I hung it in my closet when I went to bed last night, and I noticed it hanging there this morning when I dressed. But when I came up from brunch to change my outfit the evening gown wasn't hanging there any more. I ransacked the room, but it was gone."

"Who else is staying at the house?"

"Al Marsh, Johnny, of course, and the two other exes, that Kemp tramp and Miss Yokel from Wrightsville here, Alice Tierney, and what he ever saw in her—! Oh, and two characters from town who make like a maid and a butler, but they went home last night after they cleaned up. They were back this morning and I asked both of them about my gown. They looked at me as if I were out of my everloving mind."

If one of them is Morris Hunker, baby, Ellery chuckled to himself, you ain't seen nothin' yet.

"Did you ask any of the others?"

"Where do you think I'm from, Dumbsville? What good would that have done, dahling? The one who lifted it would only deny it, and the others . . . oh, it's just too embarrassing! Do you suppose I could impose on you to, well, find it for me without raising a fuss? I'd go poking around Marcia's and Alice's bedrooms, but I'd be sure to get caught, and I don't want Johnny getting, I mean thinking, well, you know what I mean, Mr. Queen."

For the sake of the amenities he was willing to concede that he did, although in truth he did not. As for the Inspector, he was watching Ellery like a psychiatrist observing if the patient would curl up in a fetal position or spring to the attack.

"Nothing else of yours was taken?"

"No, that was it. Just the gown."

"Seems to me," Inspector Queen said, "either Miss Kemp or Miss Tierney borrowed it for some reason, and if you'd just ask them—"

"I can see you don't know anything about Paris-type gowns, Inspector," the model-actress drawled. "They're like Rembrandts or something. They couldn't wear it without giving themselves away. So why take it? Y'know? That's why it's such a mystery."

"How about the maid?" Ellery asked.

"That tub? She's five-foot-two and must weigh two hundred."

"I'll see what I can do, Miss Weston," he said.

She played her exit scene seductively and with much emotion, sweeping out at last after half a dozen more "dahlings" and a long trailing goodbye arm, and leaving him with the scent of Madame Rochas Perfume for Ladies. The moment she was gone the Inspector barked, "Ellery, you're not going to start poking around for some stupid evening gown and spoil your vacation —and mine!"

"But I just promised—"

"So you're unreliable," the Inspector snorted, settling down with the Wrightsville *Record* Ellery had picked up in High Village.

"I thought you were going to take a nap."

"Who could sleep now? That phony knocked it all out of me. Now that's that, Ellery. Understand?"

But that was not that. At thirteen minutes past one the door called again, and Ellery opened to a vision in flesh, curves, and genuine red hair—a rather large vision, to be sure. She was almost as tall as Ellery, with the build of a back-row showgirl: long-muscled legs, long dancer's thighs, and a bust of Mansfieldian proportions. She was dressed for the greatest effect, in briefs and a halter, with a coat loosely open over all; it showed a great deal of her. Her flaming hair was modestly bound in a scarf.

"Marcia Kemp," Ellery said.

"Now how in Christ's name did you know that?" The redhead had a deep, coarse, New York voice—from the heart of the Bronx, Ellery guessed. Her green eyes were glittery with anger.

"I've had an advance description, Miss Kemp," Ellery said with a grin. "Come in. Meet my father, Inspector Queen of the New York City police department."

"Grandpa, fuzz is just what I need," the Kemp woman exclaimed. "You'll never guess what's happened to me. In Johnny-B's own house, mind you!"

"What was that?" Ellery asked, ignoring his father's look.

"Some creep heisted my wig."

"Your *wig?*" the Inspector repeated involuntarily.

"My green one! That piece of shrubbery set me back a whole hundred and fifty bucks. I go down to breakfast this morning, or lunch, or whatever the hell it was, and when I get back . . . *no wig!* Can you tie that? It left me so goddam uptight . . . I need a shot. Straight bourbon, Queenie baby, and lean on it."

He poured her enough bourbon to make a Kentucky colonel stagger. She tossed it down as if it were a milk shake and held the glass out for more. He refilled it. This one she nursed in her powerful hands.

"You last saw this wig of yours when, Miss Kemp?"

"I wore it last night to dinner along with my green lamé evening gown. Johnny likes his women to do the dress-up bit. It was still on my dressing table when I went downstairs this morning. When I come back it's gone with the wind. If I didn't know how Johnny hates a rumble I'd tear those bitches' luggage limb from limb! Could you find it for me, Ellery? Hush-hush, like? Without Johnny knowing?"

"There's no chance you mislaid it?" The Inspector, hopefully.

"Gramps, I ask you. How do you mislay a green wig?"

"A dress and a wig," Ellery yapped after he got rid of the redhead. "Something missing from each of the first two ex-wives. Is it possible that the third—?"

"Son, son," his father said in not entirely convincing reproof. "You promised."

"Yes, dad, but you'll have to admit . . . ."

And indeed Ellery was looking more like his old self, with a near-jaunty bounce to his step and at least a half sparkle in his eye that for some time had been missing altogether. The Inspector consoled himself with the thought that it was likely one of those pesky little problems, with the simplest of explanations, that would keep Ellery harmlessly occupied while time and river washed away the stains left by the Glory Guild case.

So when at midafternoon Ellery suddenly said, "Look, dad, if there's any logic in all this, the third one ought to be missing something, too. I think I'll stroll over . . . ," the Inspector said simply, "I'll be down at the brook with a rod, son."

Benedict had had a sixty-foot swimming pool built behind the main house. It was still covered by a winter tarpaulin; but summer furniture had been set out on the flagstoned terrace at the rear of the old farmhouse that he had had laid down in the reconstruction, and there Ellery found Alice Tierney stretched out in a lounging chair, sunning herself. The spring afternoon was warm, with a gusty little breeze, and her cheeks were reddened as if she had been lying there for some time.

The moment he laid eyes on her Ellery recognized

her. During one of his trips to Wrightsville he had had
to visit the hospital. On that occasion, attending the
object of his visit, she had been in a nurse's cap and
uniform—a large girl with a healthy butt, a torso of
noble dimensions, and features as plain as Low Village's
cobbles and as agreeable to the eye.

"Miss Tierney. I don't suppose you remember me."

"Don't I just!" she cried, sitting up. "You're the great
Ellery Queen, God's gift to Wrightsville."

"You don't have to be nasty about it," Ellery said,
slipping into a wrought-iron chair.

"Oh, but I mean it."

"You do? Who calls me that?"

"Lots of people around here." Her cool blue eyes
shimmered in the sun. "Of course, I've heard some say
the gift comes from the devil, but you'll find sourpusses
everywhere."

"That's probably because of the rise in the crime rate
since I began coming here. Smoke, Miss Tierney?"

"Certainly not. And you oughtn't to, either. Oh,
futz! There I go again. I can never forget my training."

She was in mousy slacks and jacket that did nothing
for her, and he thought her long straight hair style was
exactly wrong for her face and size. But it all tended
to dwindle away against her general air of niceness,
which he suspected she cultivated with great care.
He could understand what Johnny Benedict, with his
superficial view of women, had found so appealing
about her.

"I'm so glad you decided to come out of your shell,"
Alice Tierney went on animatedly. "Johnny threatened
us with all sorts of punishment if we didn't let you
strictly alone."

"I'm still not diving back into the drink. As a matter
of fact, I came here for only one reason: to ask what
may strike you as a peculiar question."

"Oh?" She did seem puzzled. "What's that, Mr. Queen?"

Ellery leaned toward her. "Have you missed anything today?"

"Missed? Like what?"

"Something personal. Say an article of clothing."

"No . . . ."

"You sure?"

"Well, I suppose something could be . . . I mean, I haven't taken inventory." Alice Tierney laughed, but when he did not laugh back she stopped. "You really mean it, Mr. Queen!"

"I do. Would you mind going to your room right now—quietly, Miss Tierney—and checking over your things? I'd rather no one in the house knows what you're about."

She rose, drew a breath, smoothed her jacket, then launched herself toward the house rather like an oversized missile.

Ellery waited with the patience of a thousand such interludes, when a puzzle loomed which gave off no immediate meaning, only a promise for the future.

She was back in ten minutes. "That is queer," she said, plumping back into the lounge chair. "A pair of my gloves."

"Gloves?" Ellery looked at her hands. They were big and capable-looking. "What kind of gloves, Miss Tierney?"

"Long evening gloves. White. The only such pair I had with me."

"You're sure you had them."

"I wore them to dinner last night." The red in her cheeks deepened. "Johnny prefers his women to look, oh, untouchable, I suppose it's what it is at bottom. He hates slobby-gobs."

"White evening gloves. Is anything else of yours missing?"

"Not that I know of."

"You checked?"

"I looked through everything. Why in the world should someone steal a pair of gloves? There's not much use for evening gloves in Wrightsville. Among the class of people who'd steal, I mean."

"That, of course, is the problem. Miss Tierney, I'm going to ask you to keep this to yourself. About the theft, and about the fact that I've been asking questions."

"If you say so, of course."

"By the way, where is everybody?"

"They're getting ready to drive over to the airport to pick up Al Marsh's secretary, a Miss Smith. She's due in at the field at five thirty. Annie and Morris are starting dinner in the kitchen."

"Morris Hunker?"

"Is there more than one?" Alice Tierney grinned. "You know Morris, I take it."

"Oh, yes. But who's Annie?"

"Annie Findlay."

"Findlay . . . ?"

"Her brother Homer used to run the garage down on Plum Street. You know, where High and Low sort of meet."

"Homer Findlay and his Drive Urself! For heaven's sake. How is Homer?"

"Peaceful," Miss Tierney said. "Cardiac arrest. I closed his eyes in the Emergency Room at WGH six years ago."

Ellery left, shaking his head at Old Mortality. And other things.

Inspector Queen had taken the Cougar down into town and came back chortling over a find. He had stumbled on a store, new to Ellery, which sold fresh fish and shellfish—"not frozen, mind you, son, you freeze fish, shellfish especially, and you wind up losing half the flavor. Wait till you see what I've got planned for the menu tonight."

"What, dad?"

"I said wait, didn't I? Don't be so nosy."

What his father served that evening was, he said, an "Irish bouillabaisse," which Ellery found indistinguishable from the Mediterranean variety except that it had been made by an Irishman who left out the saffron— "can't abide that yellow stuff," the chef declared. It was delicious, and Ellery gave it its due. But after dinner, when the Inspector suggested they go into town to see "one of those naked movies" (Wrightsville had acquired an art cinema), Ellery grew less communicative.

"Why don't you go see it, dad? I don't feel much like a movie tonight, even a naked one."

"Sometimes I wonder! What'll you do?"

"Oh, listen to some music. Maybe get potted on Johnny's slivovitz or akvavit or something."

"May I live to see the day," his father grumbled; and, surprisingly, he took off.

There's libido in the old boy yet, Ellery thought, and blessed it.

He had no intention of communing with Mozart or the three Bs, or the international contents of Benedict's bar. As soon as the sound of the Cougar died, Ellery slipped a dark jacket over his white turtleneck, rousted a flash from the tool room, left several lights burning in the cottage and a stereo cartridge playing, and stole outside.

There was a new moon, and the darkness was as dark only as dark can be in Wrightsville's woods. He kept his hand over the light as he walked up the path toward the main house. There was a rawness to the night; he would have welcomed a symphony of peepers, but apparently the season was too early or the

weather discouraged them, even though spring was
officially a week old. If the Inspector had been present
to ask him what he was doing, Ellery could not
honestly have answered. He had no idea what he was
about, except that he could not get the three thefts
out of his head. And since they had taken place in
Benedict's house, he was drawn there like a flower
child to a pot party.

There was something maddeningly logical about the
thefts. An evening gown, a wig *à la mode*, and evening
gloves. They went together like pieces of a jigsaw. The
difficulty was, when they were assembled they represented nothing. The three articles had some value, of
course; and, value being relative, theft for a material
reason could not be dismissed as a possibility, although
the monitor who sat deep in Ellery's brain kept shaking
its infallible little head. The obvious reason, that they
had been stolen to be worn, was even less appealing:
if the thief had been one of the ex-wives, it meant that
she had included one of her own things in order to
spread the guilty area, an absurd complexity considering the peculiar nature of the thefts; and if the thief
had not been one of the ex-wives but some woman
from Wrightsville, where could she wear the stolen
finery without becoming suspect?

Morris Hunker he eliminated without a doubt; the
old Yankee would not have taken a crust from a spar-
row if he were dying of hunger. Annie Findlay, of
course, was an unknown quantity to him, and the
simple answer might be that the roly-poly sleep-out
"maid" had been unable to resist the glittery gown, the
fantastic wig, and the—to her—unusual gloves. But Ellery had understood that, like Hunker, Annie hired out
for her livelihood to special employers like John Benedict; in a small town like this she could hardly have
indulged a regular weakness for other people's belong-
ings without long since being found out. Besides,

lightfingered hired help were practically unknown in Wrightsville. No, Annie as the culprit just didn't scan.

Then who? If it had been a prowler, surely he could have found far more valuable and negotiable pickings in the Benedict house than a second-hand gown, a green wig, and a pair of women's evening gloves (undoubtedly soiled). Yet the three women had reported nothing else missing. And certainly if Benedict or Marsh had suffered a loss, he would have heard by this time.

It was the kind of trivial-seeming puzzle that always drove Ellery to distraction.

He circled the house, choosing his path with stealth. The front and the side where the kitchen and pantry must lie showed no lights; evidently Hunker and the Findlay woman had cleaned up after dinner and gone home. But lights blazed onto the terrace through the French doors Benedict had had installed in the living room's rear wall during his reconstruction of the farmhouse.

Ellery edged onto the patio, keeping to the shadows beyond the lighted area. He chose a position under the branches of a forty-year-old pink dogwood tree very near the house, from where he could see into the living room without being seen. The room must be warm: one of the French doors was ajar. He heard their voices clearly.

They were all there: Benedict, his ex-wives, Marsh, and a girl who could only be Marsh's secretary, Miss Smith. The secretary was seated at the edge of a sofa, to one side, legs crossed, with a pad on her knee and a pencil poised; she wore a no-nonsense navy blue skirt of medium length, a tailored white blouse, and a white cardigan thrown about her shoulders and buttoned at the neck. There was nothing youthful or even womanly about her; her mechanical makeup gave her horsy face a circus precision; she was, in fact, quite masculine-looking aside from her legs, which were shaped well and surprisingly feminine. She told Ellery something about Marsh. A man who would select a Miss Smith for private secretarial chores could be relied on to reserve his office hours for business purposes exclusively.

Two of the ex-wives seemed dressed for a race, in evening getups that evoked the yachtsman's starting gun.

Audrey Weston's blonde beauty was offset by black evening pajamas and a black crepe tunic, with a broad red satin sash tied high above the waist that underscored her breasts, and needle-heeled red satin shoes that added inches to her mainmast height; she wore a bracelet of gold links that looked heavy enough to secure an anchor, and gold coil earrings.

The generally flappy, full-canvas effect of Audrey's outfit, exciting as it was, barely held its own with Marcia Kemp's. The redheaded expatriate from Las Vegas had trimmed down to the bare poles; her turquoise evening sheath was so painted to her body that Ellery wondered how she was able to sit down without cracking her hull . . . and, as a corollary, whether Benedict's wives numbers two and one had put their heads together in planning their racing strategy. Was the contest fixed?

By contrast, Alice Tierney's coloring showed darker against the whiteness of her gown and accessories; she looked pure and chaste in it, and very nearly striking. It was as if she realized that she could not by natural endowment outshine her predecessors and so had shrewdly employed a tactic of simplicity.

But if Audrey's and Marcia's calculated art and Alice's calculated artlessness were designed to stir old passions in Benedict's libido, the effects were not visible to the Queen eye. Outwardly, at least, he was as unmoved by their bountiful charms as a eunuch. If proof

of his general contempt for the trio were needed, Ellery found it in Benedict's attire. The millionaire being
so finical about his women, one would expect con-
sistency, or at least *noblesse oblige*, in the form of a
dinner jacket; but while Marsh was suitably in black
tie, Benedict was wearing an ordinary brown suit—as
if, being Johnny-B, he could afford to flout the conven-
tions he expected of his ex-wives. It made Ellery see
his old friend in a newish light.

Ellery felt no qualms at eavesdropping; he never did
when his curiosity was engaged. He had long since
had this out with himself. (He did not recommend it
as a general practise; only—as in the practise of bugging—when performed by experts for lawful purposes,
in which category he felt entitled to place himself.)

What they had been talking about before his arrival,
Ellery gathered, was "the new will" Benedict was having Marsh draw up for him "tomorrow." (So he had
not told the ex-Mrs. Benedicts of the holograph document he had signed in the Queens' presence Thursday
night, and which lay in the Inspector's pocket at this
moment.)

"But that's nothing but fraud," Audrey Weston
snarled.

"Fraud?" The redhead from Vegas uttered a four-
letter word with great sincerity. "It's murder!"

Alice Tierney looked pained.

"You know, Marcia, your vulgarity is so lacking in
originality," Marsh said from the bar, where he was
replenishing his drink. "I'll give you this, though: people know just where they stand with you at all times."

"You want me to give you a personal reading right
now, Al?"

"Heaven forbid, dear heart!" He enveloped his
drink hastily.

Ellery found himself bound to his dogwood. Fraud?
Murder? But then he decided it had been hyperbole.

"Leeches!" Benedict's sang-froid was gone. "You know damn w-well what our marriages were. Strictly business. Contracts with a m-mattress thrown in." He stabbed at them with his arms. "Well, I'm finished with that kind of stupidity!"

"Down, boy," Marsh said.

"You know our d-deal! The same in each c-case, a thousand a week, payable till your remarriages or my death; then, on my death, each of you under my will, if still not m-married"—*which will?*—"gets a settlement in a lump sum of one m-million dollars."

"Yes, but look what we signed away," Alice Tierney said in a soft and reasonable voice. "You made us sign prenuptial agreements in which we had to renounce all dower and other claims to your estate."

"Under the threat, if I recall correctly—and, brother, do I!—" Audrey Weston said caustically, "that if we didn't sign, the marriage was off."

"Sweetie," Marcia Kemp said, "that's the great Johnny-B's style."

Marsh laughed. "Still, girls, not a bad deal for leasing Johnny the use of your bodies, impressive as they are, for a few months." He had made too many trips to the bar; there was the slightest slur to his speech and a stiffness to his smile.

"Impressive is as impressive does—right, Al?" Benedict brandished a hand graceful as a dagger. "The p-point is, pets, I've been thinking a great many things over, and I've decided that with you three specimens I didn't get my m-money's worth. So I've changed my mind about the whole bit. Besides, there's a new element in the plot I'll get to in a m-minute. I'm having Al write my new w-will tomorrow, as I told you, and you can be n-nice about it or not, it's all the s-same to me."

"Hold on, dahling!" Tallu was back. "You can't

change a settlement just like that, you know. A girl scorned has some rights in Uncle Sam country!"

"I do believe you didn't read the f-fine print, Audrey," Benedict said. "The agreements in no case made your renunciation of dower rights and other claims against my estate c-contingent on what I chose to leave you in my will. Read it again, Audrey, will you? You'll save yourself an attorney's fee. Right, Al?"

"Right," Marsh said. "Also, the agreements and the will they're attached to were in no way affected by the decrees."

"And if I want to change my mind about those three millions, there's not a b-bloody thing you can do about it." Benedict displayed his teeth. "I assure you that what we're planning is p-perfectly legal. Anything that might be iffy—well, I'll match my beagle against yours on any track in the land."

"Wuff," Marsh said.

"In other words, buster," and the redhead showed *her* teeth, "you're going to the muscle."

"If I must."

"But you promised," the ex-nurse said. "Johnny, you gave me your word . . . ."

"Nonsense."

Marcia had been thinking. She lit a cigaret. "All right, Johnny, what's the new deal?"

"I'll continue to p-pay each of you a thousand per week until you remarry or I d-die, but the million-apiece lump-sum payoff on my death, that's out."

Marcia spat one word: "Why?"

"Well, it's really none of your b-business," Benedict said, "but I'm getting married again."

"You've got to be kidding," Audrey cried. "You catch a case of marriage every spring, Johnny, like a cold. What's getting remarried got to do with anything?"

"You couldn't be that mean," Alice wailed. "A million dollars is no joking matter."

"So you'll be hitched to this broad for a few months," Marcia growled, "and then—"

"This time it's d-different," Benedict said, smiling. "This time," and he stopped smiling, "I'm in love."

It was Audrey, the blonde, who shrieked, *"Love?* You?" but the incredulity might have been sounded by any of them. Then they all burst into laughter.

"Al, get him to a shrink presto," the redhead said, "before he drops what's left of his marbles. Listen, bubby, the last thing you were in love with was your mama's titty. What do you know about love?"

Benedict shrugged. "Whatever it's called, I've c-caught it. I want to settle down—go ahead and snicker!—breed a flock of kids, lead a normal l-life. No more chick-chasing or marriage quickies. My next wife is going to be the last woman in my life." They were roosting there like three birds on a perch, bills gaping. "That's the m-main reason behind this move. If I'm going to be the f-father of children, I want to secure their future. And their mother's. I'm n-not going to change my mind about that."

"I still say it's fraud," the blonde snapped. "Or was that will you showed me prior to the divorce proceeding, leaving me a million dollars—was that another con?"

"If it was, he conned me, too," Marcia barked. "And I say it again. It's plain murder to cut us off after we've given you—"

"I know, Marcia—the b-best months of your life." Benedict grinned. "You three never would let me finish a sentence. I was about to announce that this isn't going to be a total l-loss to you. What's m-more, you'll have till tomorrow noon to decide. How f-fair can a fairy god-husband get? Al, d'ye mind? A Black Russian."

It was a new one to Ellery, and he watched Marsh

busy himself at the bar. Marsh blended what appeared
to be vodka and some coffee liqueur over ice.

"Decide what, Johnny?" Alice asked in a defeated
voice.

"Tell you in a minute. The point is, if you three do
agree, Al makes out my new w-will and that will be
that."

"What—is—the—deal?" Audrey as Audrey. No stagey
nonsense now.

"A thousand a week as at p-present, with the usual
hedge in case of remarriage, and on my death each of
you receives one hundred thousand dollars. And that's
the end of the g-game as far as our foursome is concerned. Granted a hundred th-thousand isn't a million
—thank you, Al—but it's not exactly b-birdseed, either.
Even for three rare birds like you.

"So think it over, ladies. If you decide to make a
court fight of it, I tell you now before w-witnesses:
the new w-will tomorrow won't leave you a red c-cent!
I might even change my mind about the thousand a
week. Nighty night."

And John Levering Benedict III drained his Black
Russian, waved it in their general direction, set the
empty glass down, and went upstairs to bed as if he
had had an active but rewarding day.

Benedict left behind him an atmosphere of anger,
frustration, and curiosity, with curiosity dominant on
a field of gold.

"Who is this babe Johnny's going to marry?"

"Do you know? You know, goddam it!"

"Tell us, Al! Come on. . . ."

The Amazons surrounded Marsh, pushing their soft
plenitude at him.

"Please, girls, not before Miss Smith. We run a proper
ship in the home waters, don't we, Miss Smith? That's

it for tonight, by the way. You're on your own. Perfectly free to raid the kitchen if you want a snack."

"I'm on a diet," Miss Smith said unexpectedly, and the lawyer looked surprised. Ellery gathered that the personal remark was not characteristic of Miss Smith's professional behavior. She shut her stenographic book over the pencil with a little snap. "Good night, Mr. Marsh," she said emphatically, and marched upstairs as if the ex-wives had gone back into a bottle. She had taken down every word uttered in the room during Ellery's surveillance.

"I know you know who she is, Al," Audrey said, shaking him playfully.

"Is it that hatcheck broad they say he's been giving the treatment to lately?" big Marcia wanted to know.

"He wouldn't dream of making a mistake like *that* again, dear," Alice said sincerely.

"At least I never sucked blood like you did when he picked you up in this outhouse they call a town," the redhead retorted. "Bat Girl! Is there anything lower than a bloodsucker?"

"Look who's talking!"

"Come on, Al," the blonde whinnied, "stop hogging the sauce. I want a drink, dahling. And shovel us the dirt."

Marsh shook them off and walked back to the bar with his glass. "Mine not to shovel, mine but to do as I'm told. My advice to you, offered absolutely free, is to accept Johnny's offer and be damned to him. Turn it down and you'll wind up like the call girl in the gay bar—I mean to say, girls, with a handful of nothing. That hundred thousand per ex is the most you'll ever get out of Johnny, and you've got about twelve hours to grab for it. Think it over. You can verbalize your pretty little decisions to me in the morning."

"You go to hell, dahling," Audrey said. "What about my drink?"

"Why don't you go to bed?"

"I'm not desperate enough. Oh, all right, I'll get it myself." The blonde actress got up and sauntered to the bar.

"You know what you are?" Marcia said to the lawyer in an even voice. "You're a lousy brown-nose. Mix me a gibson, will you, Audrey?"

"Mix it yourself."

"You're a charmer. Don't think I won't." The redhead joined the blonde at the bar.

"Al . . . ," the brunette from Wrightsville began.

"You won't get any more out of me than they did, Alice. Good night."

"You can't dismiss me as if I were Miss Smith! Or a child." Alice gave him a cold and thoughtful look on her way to the bar.

Ellery was more intent on observing Marsh. Marsh had evidently had enough alcohol for the moment; the glass he set down was more than half full. But he was continuing to smoke full blast. He had been chain-smoking menthol cigarets ever since Ellery began to eavesdrop, and he was chainsmoking them still. Well, Ellery thought, being legal eagle as well as companion and confidant to a man like Johnny-B did not exactly make for an untroubled existence. The Marlboro man sitting his faithful steed might well develop, along with calluses, a neurosis or two. Even agoraphobia.

Ellery studied the heavy male features and the big and sensitive hands, and he wondered if Marsh had any notion of the can of peas his friend and client had so blithely opened. Marsh's intelligence had been systematized by his legal training; surely he must be able to analyze the possibilities. Well, perhaps not surely. He hasn't had my conditioning in murder, Ellery thought. It takes experience and a soiled mind to think of a thing like that.

He slid off the terrace, and on his way back to the

cottage—using the flashlight sparingly—Ellery let conditioning take charge. His thoughts did not provoke, amuse, or engross him. The exercise, as usual, was futile. The trouble with foreseeing homicide on the sole ground of past performances was that there was no profit in it. The victim was never convinced before it was too late for convincing, and warning off the potential murderers either spurred them to a more cunning crime or planted an unsocial thought where none had been. The victim, like all mortals, assumed that he was immortal, and the murderer, like most murderers, that he was infallible. Against these diseases there was no specific.

It was all very sad and discouraging; and Ellery was grumbling away in his sleep before Inspector Queen got back from his movie.

It came off on schedule, almost as if Ellery had planned it.

He groped for the light-chain at the eruption of the telephone, found it, dragged it, blinked at his watch and noted the time as 3:03 A.M., fumbled about for the phone and found that—all before he was really awake. But the gasp and heave in his ear were like a wash of seawater.

"Who is this?"

"J-J-J . . . ."

"Johnny? Is this Johnny?"

"Yes." He was hauling the breath from his lungs as if it had weights attached. "El . . . ?"

"Yes, yes, what's wrong?"

"Dying."

"You? Wait! I mean, I'll be right over."

"No . . . time."

"Hang on—"

"M-m-m . . . ." He stopped. There was a gurgly

sob. Then Benedict said, "Murder," in a quite ordinary
way.

Ellery said swiftly, "Who, Johnny? Tell me. Who
did it?"

This time the dragged-out breath, interminable.

And Johnny Benedict said distinctly, "Home," and
stopped again.

Ellery found himself irritated. Why does he want
me to know where he is? I know where he is. Or must
be. At the main house. Using the extension. It made
no sense. He was making no sense. If he could call me,
he could be lucid. He had no right to be out of his
head—to go this far only to tell me he was calling from
home.

"I mean, who attacked you?"

He heard some meaningless sounds. It was exasper-
ating.

"Hold on, Johnny, hold on! Who did it?" It was like
trying to coax a recalcitrant child. "Try to tell me." He
almost said "daddy" instead of the pronoun.

Johnny tried, according to his lights. He was on the
"home" kick again. He said it three times, each time
less distinctly, less assertively, with more of a stam-
mer. Finally he stopped trying and there was nothing
but a defeated *thunk!* at the other end, the phone hit-
ting something, as if Johnny-B had flung it away or,
what was less pleasantly probable, had dropped it.

"What is it, son?"

Ellery hung up. To his surprise, he found himself
yawning. It was his father, in the doorway. The Inspector did not sleep well any more. The least interruption in the rhythm of his environment disturbed him.

"Ellery?"

He told the Inspector what Johnny had said.

"Then what are you standing here for?" the old man
yelled, and dived for his bedroom.

There's no hurry, Ellery thought as he hurriedly

pulled on his pants. Johnny's gone with the wind he sowed.

Wrightsville strikes again.

The Cougar covered the quarter mile in nothing flat. The main house was dark except for two windows upstairs which they took to be in Benedict's room, the master bedroom. Ellery jumped out, and the Inspector cried, "Did you remember to bring that key Benedict gave you?" to which Ellery replied, "Hell, no, I forgot it. Who ever used a key in Wrightsville?" and was immediately vindicated, because the front door, while it was closed, was not locked.

They ran upstairs. The master bedroom door stood open.

Benedict was in puce-colored silk pajamas, a milk-chocolate-striped silk kimono, and Japanese slippers. He lay in a heap on the floor beside the bed and he looked like a cake just out of the oven, decorated, and set aside to cool. The cradle of the telephone was on the nightstand; the receiver dangled to the floor. There was amazingly little blood, considering the wounds in Benedict's head.

The weapon lay on the floor six feet from the body, between the bed and the doorway. It was an oversized, heavy-looking Three Monkeys sculpture in a modern elongated style, cast in iron. Both the material and the stylistic distortion gave its familiar "see no evil, hear no evil, speak no evil" homily an irony terribly grotesque. Neither man touched it.

"He's dead, of course," Ellery said.

"What do you think?"

"For the record." Ellery's lips were tight. "We'd better verify."

The Inspector squatted and felt Benedict's carotid.

"He's dead. What I can't understand is where he found the strength to pick up a phone."

"He obviously found it," Ellery said coldly. "The point is: having found it, what did he do with it? Not a damned thing!"

And in an aggrieved way he wrapped a handkerchief around his right hand, picked up the receiver, punched the button on the cradle for an outside line, and from too, too solid memory dialed the number of Wrightsville police headquarters.

"It's going to be some time before Newby gets here," Ellery remarked to his father, replacing the phone. "Which is probably just as well. By the way, these guests of Johnny's sleep like the dead. Maybe we'd better check their carotids, too."

"Let 'em be," the Inspector growled. "Their time is coming. What do you mean 'just as well'?"

"The night desk man, a fellow named Peague—I'm betting he's related to Millard Peague, who used to have the locksmith shop on Crosstown and Foaming—says the chief went to a Red Man blast tonight and just got into the sack, so he won't appreciate having to get up and come out here. The three radio cars on the graveyard tour are all over at Fyfield Gunnery School—some students got high on speed or something and they're wrecking the administration building. It's developed into a full-scale engagement—state police, patrol cars from Slocum as well as Wrightsville—the locals won't be able to get here for hours, Peague says. While we're waiting for Newby we may as well make ourselves useful."

The Inspector looked doubtful. "I hate cutting in on another cop's turf."

"Newby won't mind. The Lord of battles knows we've charged shoulder to shoulder often enough. Let's see if we can find any writing materials."

"What for?"

"Superman or not, Johnny'd have written something

in preference to phoning—if he could. My hunch is we'll find nothing."

They found nothing. It gave Ellery a small satisfaction.

One mystery was solved. On the opposite side of the room from the windows, helter-skelter on the floor as if thrown there, they found the three articles of clothing Benedict's ex-wives had reported missing: Audrey Weston's black sequined gown, Marcia Kemp's green wig, and Alice Tierney's white evening gloves.

Ellery examined them eagerly. The evening gown was long enough to trail on the floor; the wig was not only absurdly green but distended—it looked like an excited hedgehog; the gloves were of high-quality kid. None of the three showed even a pinpoint of bloodstain.

"So they weren't being used at the time of the assault," the Inspector mused. "A plant?"

"Three plants," Ellery said, squinting. "Otherwise why leave all three? If Johnny's assailant had wanted to implicate Marcia, he'd have left just the wig. Or Audrey, just the gown. Or Alice, just the gloves. By leaving all three he implicates all three."

"But why?"

"That is the question."

"But I don't get it, Ellery."

"I wish I could enlighten you. I don't, either."

"Something tells me we should have stood in Manhattan," the Inspector said gloomily.

The bed had been slept in; the spread had been neatly folded at the foot, the bottom sheet was wrinkled, and the pillow still showed the depression made by Benedict's head.

"He certainly didn't go to bed with his robe on," Ellery said. "That means something woke him up, and he jumped out of bed and slipped into his robe and slippers. So the next question is: what disturbed him?"

"No sign of a struggle," the Inspector nodded. "It's as if the killer didn't want to spoil the neatness of the room."

"You're getting whimsical, dad."

"No, I mean it. No clothes thrown about, chair as naked as a jaybird, and I'll bet if you look in that hamper you'll find . . . ." Inspector Queen darted into the bathroom and yanked up the cover of the laundry hamper, which was just visible from the foot of Benedict's bed. He exclaimed in triumph, "What did I tell you? Shirt, socks, underwear—neatly deposited before he went to bed."

The Inspector came out and looked about. "He must have been left for dead, Ellery—on the bed or floor—and when the killer was gone, Benedict somehow found the moxie to crawl to the phone and call you."

"Agreed," Ellery said. "Also, from the absence of a struggle I'm tempted to conclude that Johnny knew his assailant. Although, of course, it could have been a housebreaker or other stranger who jumped him and got in an incapacitating blow just after Johnny got out of bed and put his robe and slippers on. That's one of those alternatives you never quite eliminate."

"But what did he kill him for?" The Inspector was going through the elephant-ear wallet lying on the nightstand. The wallet was fat, like the craw of a Strasbourg goose. The Rolex watch with the matching bracelet beside the wallet was an 18-carat gold, 30-jewel affair that must have set Benedict back over a thousand dollars.

"For money, that's what for," Ellery said. "But not the kind of goose feed you tote around. I went to bed worrying about exactly that. What's this?"

"This" was a walk-in wardrobe closet. The Queens walked in and routinely took inventory. Hanging on racks, with the neatness of a tailor's shop, were a dozen or so custom-made suits in fabulous fabrics and numer-

ous shades of blue and gray; two summer dinner jackets, one white, the other burgundy; a variety of pastel-
hued slacks and sports jackets; a white yachting uniform, hound's-tooth golf togs, a brown plaid hunting
and fishing outfit; four topcoats, in charcoal gray, light
gray, gabardine tan, and chocolate; three overcoats,
one black with a velvet collar, another navy blue
double-breasted, the third a casual tan cashmere. The
shoe racks held dozens of pairs of shoes—conventionals,
cordovans, alligators, suèdes, two-tones; an assortment
of boots and athletic shoes; blacks and browns and
grays and tans and oxbloods. On an upper shelf lay
ten hats and caps, from a black homburg to a severe
dark brown fedora, through the well-dressed man's Al-
pine, woodsman, and other sporty styles. An enormous
revolving rack offered a selection of four-in-hand neckties, ascots, bow ties, and scarves in all the basic solid
colors, in combinations, and in a range of materials and
designs that would not have disgraced Sulka's.

The Inspector marveled. "Why in God's name did he
need all these duds? In Wrightsville, of all places?"

"And this is just a hideaway," Ellery pointed out,
"where he apparently did little entertaining and no visiting. Imagine what the closets in his New York, Paris,
and other apartments must look like."

The bureau was a built-in affair with haberdasher's
drawers stacked with custom-made shirts of every description: broadcloths, Pimas, silks, synthetics; in
whites, blues, browns, tans, grays, greens, pinks, even
lavenders, in solids and in pinstripes; with button cuffs
and French cuffs; with dress collars and buttoned-
down collars; including a collection of plaids and
flannels and other outdoorsy items, and another of
frilled and lacy as well as conventional summer dress
shirts. Several drawers turned up a selection of knit-
wear. Others held T-shirts and shorts by the dozens,
chiefly of silk, and handkerchiefs functional and orna-

mental. And in one lay a shop-sized stock of hose, in
woolens, lisles, nylons, silks; in blacks, browns, grays,
blues; in solids and in combinations. And, of course, a
jewelry drawer for a collection of tie clasps, tackpins,
cufflinks, and other essentials of the bureau.

The Inspector kept shaking his head. Ellery's remained at rest, all but his eyes, which reflected a puzzle
of some sort.

It was as if he had mislaid something, but could
remember neither what it was nor where he had mislaid it.

Waiting for Chief Newby, the Queens went about
rousing Benedict's guests. The reason for the undis-
turbed sleep of the ex-wives and Marsh was detectable
at once by anyone with less than a severe cold. The air
in the bedrooms was sour with alcohol; evidently the
three divorcees and the lawyer had done some serious
extracurricular drinking after Ellery's departure from
his eavesdropping post on the terrace. They were a
little stubborn about waking up.

As for Miss Smith, Marsh's secretary, she had locked
her bedroom door, and Ellery had to pound for several
minutes before she responded. There were no fumes
in her room. "I sleep like the dead," Miss Smith said—a
figure of speech she clearly regretted a moment later
when he told her why he had roused her. From the
noises immediately emanating from her bathroom, Miss
Smith was paying the price the three other women
should have paid but had not. Ellery left her to fortify
her rebellious stomach.

As far as he and his father could make out, Marcia
Kemp, Audrey Weston, and Alice Tierney greeted the
news of Benedict's violent death with stupefaction.
They seemed too stunned to grasp the implications;
there were no hysterics and very few questions. As for
Marsh, he gaped at the Queens from a graying face,

his big hands trembling. "Are the police here yet?" he asked; and Ellery said, "On their way, Al," whereupon the lawyer sat down on the bed mumbling, "Poor old Johnny, what a stinking deal," and asked if he might have a drink. Ellery brought him a bottle and a glass; Inspector Queen warned the quintet to remain where they were, each in his own room, and took up a sentry post at the door of Benedict's bedroom; and that was all.

Ellery was downstairs waiting for Newby when the chief—tieless, a topcoat thrown over his uniform—stalked into the house.

Anselm Newby had succeeded Chief Dakin, who personified law and order in Wrightsville for so long that only the thinning ranks of oldtimers remembered his predecessor, a fat, spittoon-targeting ex-farmer named Horace Swayne. Dakin, who always reminded Ellery of Abe Lincoln, had been the old-fashioned small-town incorruptible policeman; Anse Newby was of the new breed, young, aggressive, and scientifically trained on a city-sized police force. He was a ball of fire where Dakin had been a plodder, yet he had had to prove himself a dozen times over before the town would grudgingly grant that he might be able to fill part of old Dakin's size-13 shoes. Newby's fate it was to be a small, delicate-appearing man in a community where any suspicion of effeminacy was hated rather than despised, and in a police chief was considered a crime in itself. He soon disabused the town on this score. When the rumors reached his ears he tracked them to their source, shucked his uniform jacket, and administered a scientific beating to the offender—who had a six-inch height and thirty-five-pound weight advantage—that was the talk of Wrightsville's bars for many years. With this demonstration of his masculinity Newby had no further trouble with rumormongers. And with his stinging voice and eyes of inorganic blue, unwinking as mineral, he tended to grow on people, not always pleasantly.

"Sorry about this, Chief—" Ellery began, not altogether humorously.

"You're always sorry about this," Newby snapped. "I'm suggesting to the First Selectman that he haul arse on up to the capital and see if he can't talk our assembly-man into pushing a bill through the legislature putting Wrightsville off limits to anybody named Queen. Can't you set foot in this town without causing a homicide? I didn't know you were visiting, or I'd have put out an A.P.B. on you! How are you, Ellery?"

"I feel as rotten about it as you, Anse," Ellery said, pumping the delicate hand. "Rottener. I purposely kept our visit quiet—"

"Our? Who'd you come up with?"

"My dad. He's upstairs keeping an eye on Bene-dict's room and the body. We're here on a rest cure. On Johnny Benedict's invitation."

"Father or not, he probably doesn't know your Wrightsville record as well as I do, or he'd never have come. For a cop to take a vacation with you is a bus-man's holiday for sure. And look what Benedict's invite got *him*. Well, tell me about this one, you hoodoo."

"Let's go up."

Upstairs, the Inspector and Newby shook hands like adversaries; they had never met. But when the old man said, "I hope you don't mind our poking around while we waited for you, Chief. I don't care much my-self for police officers who stick their noses into other men's territory," Newby warmed perceptibly. "Mighty lucky for me you were here, Inspector," he said, and Ellery let his breath go.

It took the best part of forty-five minutes to brief the Wrightsville chief on the marital and testamentary situ-ations that had presumably led to Benedict's murder, while Newby examined the body and the premises.

"I left orders to get my tech men out of bed," Newby said. "Where the hell are they? Ellery, d'ye mind? Fetch those five people down here while I notify the coroner's doc to climb out of his sack and bring his tail over here. We just don't have the kind of setup and manpower you're used to, Inspector," he said in what sounded like an apology, and he made for the telephone in the foyer.

"He seems to think he has to put a show on for me," the Inspector remarked to Ellery.

Ellery grinned, "I didn't realize Anse was that human," and hurried upstairs.

The five trooped into the living room in a symbiosis of reluctance and relief. None of them had been told more than the unembellished fact of Benedict's murder; each having been isolated from the others, they had had no opportunity to exchange speculations or recriminations or to compare stories; they were all, in the flamboyant word of the times, uptight. Even more interesting, the ex-wives tended to cluster together where before Benedict's death they had staked out independent territories in the living room.

As for Miss Smith, not unexpectedly after her exhibition of secretarial aloofness, she showed signs of strain. The bout with her stomach had left her pale and ill. She mewed for a brandy, at which Marsh, even in his preoccupation, looked astonished. And she kept babbling away in a complaining voice, principally to Marsh, as if the predicament in which she found herself was all her employer's fault. At least four times she whined, "I've never had anything to do with a murder before," as if he had dragged her into something very common in his set; until Marcia Kemp tossed her red locks and said grimly, "Oh, for chrissake, shut *up*," at which Miss Smith looked frightened, clutched her brandy, and subsided.

"Now look, folks," Newby said when the Inspector had identified the five. "I know darned little about this setup, though I guarantee you I'll know a lot more about it before I'm through. But as of this minute I have no notion who killed Mr. Benedict. So that's our first order of business. Anybody here got anything to tell me that's going to cut our work down?"

No one seemed able or prepared to do so. Until finally Marsh said in a voice as gray as his face, "Surely, Chief, you can't believe anyone here had anything to do with Johnny's death?"

"All right, that formality's out of the way. Anybody hear anything after getting to bed? An argument, a fight? Or even just footsteps?"

No one had. Deep sleep had been the order of the night during the period of the murder (they claimed at first), in the main induced by bourbon and vodka. Except, again, in Miss Smith's case. (Miss Smith did not "drink"—she placed audible quotation marks around the word. The brandy in her clutch was for restorative purposes.)

The ex-Mrs. Benedicts, it seemed, had originally found sleep elusive. Freshly bedded, they said, they had been wakeful.

"I tossed and tossed," Audrey Weston said. "So I thought if maybe I did some reading. You know." (Ellery waited for her to add "dahling," but the blonde seemed to realize that Chief Newby would not take kindly to the endearment.) "I came downstairs and got a book."

"Where downstairs, Miss Weston?" Newby asked.

"This room. From those bookshelves there."

"Was anybody down here while you were?"

"No."

"How long did you stay?"

"Just long enough to pick out a book."

"Then you went back upstairs?"

"That's right."

"How long did you read, Miss Weston, before you tried to get to sleep again?"

"I found I couldn't. The type began swimming before my eyes."

"Which book was it?" Ellery asked.

"I don't recall the title," the blonde said haughtily. "Something—the latest—by that Roth person."

"Philip Roth?"

"I think that's his Christian name."

"Harry Golden will be delighted to hear it. The title wasn't *Portnoy's Complaint*, was it?"

Miss Weston grew haughtier. "I'd forgotten."

"Miss Weston, if you'd begun *Portnoy's Complaint*, I don't believe the type would have swum before your eyes. The fact is you read for some time, didn't you?"

"The fact is, *dahling*," Audrey Weston spat, "I was so absolutely *revolted* I threw the disgusting thing across the room! Then I went downstairs for another book, and I got one, and started to read *that*, but that was when the sauce hit me and I got very sleepy all of a sudden, so I put out the light and the next thing I knew I was out of this world. And don't ask me what the other book was, Mr. Queen, because I haven't *any* recollection. It's still in my room if you think it's important."

"So you made two trips downstairs during the night."

"If you don't believe me, that's your problem."

"It may well be yours," Ellery said thoughtfully, and stepped back with a wave to Newby. "Didn't mean to monopolize, Anse. Go ahead."

"What time was it, Miss Weston, when all this happened?"

"I haven't the foggiest."

"No idea at all?"

"I wasn't watching clocks."

"Not even your wristwatch when you undressed?"

"I just didn't."

"Can't you make a guess what time it was? One? Two? Three?"

"I don't know, I tell you. Marcia, what time did I go up to bed?"

"You answer your questions, dearie," Marcia Kemp said, "and I'll answer mine."

"I'll tell you what time it was when you went up to bed," Alice Tierney said suddenly. "It was just about two."

"It couldn't have been that late!" Audrey cried.

"Well, it was."

"You tossed and tossed," Newby said, "then you went downstairs for *Portnoy's Complaint,* which you read for how long?"

"Really," the blonde said. "I wasn't counting. A short while."

"Fifteen minutes? A half hour?"

"Maybe. I don't know."

"Or an hour?" Ellery murmured.

"No! Closer to a half hour."

"In other words, Mr. Roth's opus revolted but held you for a half hour or more. I got the impression from what you said before that you'd hardly begun reading when you flung the book aside in disgust. You're really not making very responsive answers."

"Why are you after me, Mr. Queen?" the blonde cried. "What are you, out to get me or something? All right, I read that foul book a good long time, and the second one I hardly glanced at. But it all comes out the same at the end, because I was fast asleep *long* before whoever killed Johnny killed him."

Newby pounced. "How do you know when Benedict was killed, Miss Weston? No one here mentioned it."

She was stricken. "Didn't . . . ? Well . . . I mean, I just assumed . . . ."

He let it go. "Did you happen to see anyone on your trip downstairs or on your way back up? Either time?"

"Nobody. The bedroom doors were all shut, by the way, as far as I could see. I naturally thought everyone but me was asleep."

Newby said suddenly, "How about you, Miss Kemp?"

But she was ready for him. "How about me?"

"Did you fall right asleep when you went up to bed?"

"I wish I could say I did," the redhead answered, "but something tells me when you've got nothing to hide in a case like this it's better to tell the truth, the whole truth, and nothing but the truth. I'd had a real snootful down here and I didn't think I'd make it to the hay, I was so rocky. But I no sooner hit the bed than I was wide awake—"

"Hold it. What time was it when you left to go to bed?"

"I was in no condition to tell time, Chief. All I know is it was after Audrey went upstairs."

"How long after?"

Marcia Kemp shrugged.

"I can tell you," Alice Tierney said, "It was close to two thirty."

"You li'l ol' timekeeper, you," the redhead growled. "Anyway, my head was spinning, and I thought food might settle my stomach down, so I went downstairs to the kitchen and made myself a dry chicken sandwich and a cup of warm milk and brought them back up to my room. Grandpa there spotted the plate with the crumbs on it and the dirty glass when he woke me up a while back. Tell 'em, Grandpa."

"I saw the plate and the glass, yes," Inspector Queen said. He had been standing by the French doors overlooking the terrace, keeping himself out of the way.

"See?" Marcia said. She was wearing a shortie nightgown under her negligee, and the negligee kept coming apart. Ellery found himself wishing she would fasten it so that he could keep his mind on the testimony. Under the translucent stuffs she appeared like a giant flower about to burst into blossom. "The warm milk must have done it because after a while I corked off. I didn't know a blessed other thing until old fuzz there woke me up."

"Did you happen to see anyone during your trip to the kitchen and back?"

"No."

"I suppose you didn't hear anything around the time of the murder, either?"

"You're not catching me, buster. I don't know when the time of the murder was. Anyway, I didn't hear anything *any* time."

Alice Tierney's difficulty had been the alcohol, too. "I'm not much of a drinker," the Wrightsville ex-nurse said, "and I'd had a few too many last night. I went up to my room after Marcia, and when I couldn't fall asleep I crawled to the bathroom for something for my head. I couldn't find aspirin or anything in the medicine chest, so I went to the downstairs lavatory where I'd noticed some Bufferin during the day. I swallowed a couple and went back to my room. The Bufferin didn't help much, so I tried cold compresses. Finally out of desperation I took a sleeping pill from a bottle I found in the medicine chest—I hate sleeping pills, I've had too much experience with them—and that did it. I went out cold." Like Audrey and Marcia, Alice had seen no one and heard nothing.

"Funny," Chief Newby remarked. "With all that cross traffic up and down the stairs last night, you'd think somebody would have run into somebody. How about you, Mr. Marsh? What did you go traipsing downstairs for?"

"I didn't. Once I got to my room I stayed there. I had more than my quota last night, too, especially after Johnny went up to bed. I don't think I was conscious for two minutes after my head hit the pillow. The next thing I knew Ellery was shaking me."

"What time did you go up to bed?"

"I don't know exactly. My impression is it was right after Alice Tierney, but I'm fuzzy about it."

"No, that's right," the Wrightsville girl said.

"And you, Miss Smith?"

Challenged by name Miss Smith started, slopping what was left in her snifter. "I can't imagine why you should question me at all! I don't think I ever said more than a hello to Mr. Benedict when he visited Mr. Marsh's office."

"Did you leave your room last night after you went to bed?"

"I did not!"

"Did you hear anything that might help us, Miss Smith? Try to remember."

"I told Mr. Queen before you got here, Chief Newby, I sleep very soundly." ("Like the dead," Ellery reminded her silently.) "I thought I might have a busy day Sunday and I need my sleep if I'm to function efficiently. After all, I wasn't invited to this house as a guest. I'm here only because I'm Mr. Marsh's secretary."

"Miss Smith can't have anything to do with this," Marsh said. He said it rather harshly, Ellery thought. "I don't mean to tell you your business, Chief, but isn't all this a waste of time? Johnny must have been killed by some housebreaker who got in during the night to steal something and lost his head when Johnny woke up and surprised him."

"I wish it were that simple, Mr. Marsh." Newby glanced at Ellery. Ellery promptly went out and came back with the sequined gown, the wig, and the evening gloves.

"Since you're all Mrs. Benedicts," Ellery said to the ex-wives, "from here on in I'm going to make it easier on us by addressing you by your given names. Audrey, you came to me yesterday afternoon to report the theft of a gown from your room. Is this the one?"

He offered the black dress to the blonde. She examined it suspiciously. Then she got up slowly and fitted it to herself. "It looks like it . . . I suppose it is . . . yes. Where did you find it?"

Ellery took it from her.

"Marcia, is this the wig you told me yesterday somebody stole from your room?"

"You know it. If there's another green wig in this town I'll eat it." The redhead slipped it over her boyish crop. "This is it, all right."

"Alice, these evening gloves?"

"There was a slight nick in the forefinger of the left hand," the brunette said. "Yes, here it is. These are mine, Mr. Queen. But who had them?"

"We don't know who had them," Newby said, "but we know where they wound up. We found them in Benedict's bedroom, near his body."

This remark produced an almost weighable silence.

"But what does it mean?" Alice exclaimed. "Why should somebody steal my gloves and then leave them practically on Johnny's corpse?"

"Or my evening gown?"

"Or my kook wig?"

"I don't understand any part of this." Marsh was back at the bar, but he was paying no attention to the glass in his hand. "This sort of thing is your dish of blood, Ellery. What's it all about? Or don't you agree a burglar, or maybe a tramp—?"

"I'm afraid I don't," Ellery said. "There is a bit of sense to be made out of it, though, Al, and that's where you come in."

"Me?"

"Anse, do you mind?"

Newby shook his head. "You know more about this setup than I do, Ellery. Forget the protocol."

"Then let me shortcut this," Ellery said. "I was out on the terrace listening when Johnny made that speech last night about his intention to write a new will. I assume, Al, that since you were the lawyer who drafted Johnny's original will—the one extant when he came up here the other day—and the purpose of the weekend was to write a new will, you brought a copy of the old one along with you?"

"Yes." Marsh's tough jaw was belligerent. "You were eavesdropping, Ellery? Why?"

"Because I was uneasy about Johnny's situation, and events have borne it out. I'd like to see the will in your possession."

Marsh set his glass down on the bar. His jaw had not declared a truce. "Technically, I can refuse—"

"We know what you can do, Mr. Marsh," the chief said with a twitch of the whiplash. "But up here we aren't so formal in murder investigations. In my territory, Mr. Marsh, murder opens up a lot of doors. Let's see Benedict's will, please."

The lawyer hesitated. Finally he shrugged. "It's in my attaché case. In my room. Miss Smith—"

"Never mind," Inspector Queen said. "I'll get it."

They had forgotten he was there. He was out and back in the same unobtrusive way. "For the record, Mr. Marsh, I didn't open it."

Marsh gave him a queer look. He opened the case and drew out a thick folded document in a parchment slipcase. This he handed to Newby, who drew out the will, riffled through its numerous pages, and passed it to Ellery, who spent rather more time on it.

"I see that the basic will was drawn up a long time ago, Al, with supplementary sections added after each marriage and divorce."

"That's right."

"And according to the additions, the weekly payments to each divorced wife of a thousand dollars stop on Johnny's death but the will leaves her, if unmarried at such time, a principle sum of a million dollars as a final settlement."

"Yes."

"Then each ex-wife," Ellery said, "had a million dollars' worth of vested interest in seeing that this will remained in force until Johnny died."

"That's a rather funny way to put it, but I suppose so, yes. What's the point?"

"Oh, come, Al, I know a lawyer of your standing and background doesn't like to be mixed up in a nastiness like this, but you're in it and you'd better face up to the fact. What I overheard from the terrace last night, in the light of what subsequently happened, confirms every fear I've had. If Johnny'd survived the night, he intended to write a new will today. The new will, he said, while it would continue these ladies' thousand a week till their remarriage, at his death would cut their settlements from a million to a hundred thousand—a mere ten percent of what they could figure on collecting if he didn't or wasn't able to write the new will. And if they contested, he warned them, he wouldn't leave them a cent. I ask you, Al: From Audrey's, Marcia's, and Alice's standpoints, wasn't it a lucky break that Johnny failed to live through the night?"

Marsh gulped his drink. And the subjects of Ellery's soliloquy sat so very still they scarcely disturbed the flight of the molecules in their vicinity.

"So the way it looks," Chief Newby announced in the hush, "You used-to-be-wives of Benedict's had motive and opportunity—equal motive and opportunity. And, I might add, equal access to the murder weapon."

"I don't even know what the weapon was!" Audrey Weston, leaping. "You didn't tell us. For God's sake, I couldn't commit murder. Maybe Alice Tierney could— nurses get used to blood. But it makes me *sick* . . . ."

"I'll remember that, Audrey," Alice said in a hypodermic voice.

"For nine hundred thousand dollars, Miss Weston," the chief remarked, "most anybody could commit most anything. And oh, yes. Your evening gown was found on the scene of the crime."

"But I told Mr. Queen yesterday that it was stolen from me!" she wailed. "You found Alice's gloves and Marcia's wig up there, too, didn't he say? Why pick on me?"

"I'm not, Miss Weston. Whatever applies in this case applies to all three of you. So far. I grant you, finding all those articles in Benedict's room doesn't add up. But there they were, and juries tend to go not by fancy figuring but by plain facts."

"There's a fact in this case none of you knows," Ellery said. "Dad?"

Inspector Queen stepped forward. "On Thursday night—that was before any of you people came up here —Benedict dropped in on Ellery and me at the guest house. He told us that Marsh was going to write a new will for him over the weekend, but that, wanting to protect himself in the meantime, he'd drawn up the substance of it in his own hand and he wanted us to witness it."

The old man produced the long envelope Benedict had consigned to his care.

"My son and I watched Benedict sign and date this holograph will, we signed as witnesses, he slipped it into this envelope, and he asked me to keep it for him temporarily."

"We don't know what's in the holograph," Ellery said "—he didn't let us read it, or read it to us—but we assume it sets forth the same provisions as the one he intended Al Marsh to put in more formal language today. Under the circumstances, Anse, I believe you have every right to open it here and now."

The Inspector handed the envelope to Newby, who glanced at Marsh. Marsh shrugged and said, "You've made it clear where the local law stands, Chief," and stepped over to the bar to refill his glass.

"Did Benedict say anything to you about writing out the new will himself in advance of the weekend, Mr. Marsh?" Newby asked.

"Not a word." Marsh took a he-man swallow and flourished the glass. "Come to think of it, though, he did ask me some questions about phraseology and form in the case of a holograph will. It didn't occur to me he was seriously asking for himself."

Newby slit the envelope with his penknife and withdrew the handwritten will. The Queens rubbernecked. As they read, the three men looked increasingly surprised and puzzled.

The chief said abruptly, "You'd best take a look at this, Mr. Marsh."

Newby waved the crowding ex-wives back and offered the document to Marsh, who handled the paper, his glass, and a smoldering cigaret like a boy learning to juggle. Finally he set glass and cigaret down, and read.

He, too, looked puzzled.

"Read it aloud, Al." Ellery was watching Audrey, Marcia, and Alice. The trio were craning like giraffes. "Just that pertinent paragraph."

Marsh frowned. "He revokes all previous wills—the usual thing—and leaves his residuary estate quote 'to Laura and any children' unquote. He goes on: 'If for any reason I am not married to Laura at the time of my death, I bequeath my residuary estate to my only living kin, my first cousin Leslie.' That's the gist of it." The lawyer shrugged. "It's sloppily drawn, but in my judgment this is a legal will." He returned it to Newby and retrieved his glass and cigaret.

"Laura," Marcia muttered. "Who the hell is Laura?"

"It couldn't be that hatcheck number he's been seen with lately," Audrey said. "From what the columns have been spilling, her name is Vincentine Astor."

Alice said, "He's never mentioned a Laura to me."

"Or me," Audrey complained. "Is it possible that two-

legged rat got married secretly before he came up
here?"

"No," Ellery said. "Because in that event he'd probably have written that he was leaving his estate to 'my
wife Laura,' the common form, rather than simply 'to
Laura.' If he died before he married her, the phrase
'my wife Laura' on a will predating the marriage might
well invalidate the document and toss a will case in-
volving millions into the surrogate's court for years. No,
Johnny was anticipating his marriage to Laura—'if for
any reason I am not married to Laura,' etcetera, tells us
that. Al, do you know who Laura is, or might be?"

"He never mentioned a woman of that name to me."

"I agree with you, Ellery," Chief Newby said. "He
meant to marry this Laura right off and figured he'd
jump the gun by writing her into his interim will beforehand. He protected himself by that 'if for any
reason' clause. He must have been awfully sure of her."

"It's a tough, tough world for poor old Laura," Marcia said with a laugh that was more of a bray. "Whoever knocked Johnny off did her out of a load of rice,
Russian sable, square-cut emeralds, and Paris originals."

"Absolutely correct," Ellery said. "She won't inherit
now, whoever she is. The estate goes to Johnny's cousin.
Who is Leslie, Al, do you know?"

"Leslie Carpenter. Everyone else in both the Benedict
and Carpenter families is gone. I'll have to notify Leslie
about this right away."

"Read the part about our hundred thousand dollars,
Mr. Newby," Alice said.

Newby glanced at the will in his hand. "I can't."

"What do you mean?"

"This will doesn't mention you or Miss Kemp or Miss
Weston. There's nothing in it about leaving you a hundred thousand dollars apiece. Or ten dollars." After the
shrieks died the chief said, "It figures. He wasn't going

to commit himself on paper to you ladies for one red cent beforehand."

"That was smart of Johnny," Marsh said with a laugh.

"Shrewd would be the word," Ellery said. "He meant to propose a deal, as he subsequently did, and he saw no reason to settle his part of the bargain before you had a chance to settle yours. Also, at the time he wrote this will out I imagine his only concern was the protection of Laura or Leslie."

"In other words," said the Inspector's dry voice, "if one of you ladies knocked Benedict off, all you're going to get out of it is a choice of your last meal."

Newby's tech men and the coroner's physician drove up then, with the lightening sky, and the chief sent the ex-Mrs. Benedicts, Miss Smith, and Marsh back to their rooms and sought the phone to notify the Wright County prosecutor and the sheriff's office. The Queens left for a few hours' sleep.

Driving slowly back to the cottage in the damp dawn, Ellery said with a scowl, "I wonder how right Marsh is about that holograph will standing up."

"You told me he knows his business," the Inspector said, "so his opinion ought to be worth something. But you know how these multimillion will cases go, Ellery. Those three are sure to find hungry lawyers who for a big contingency fee will tie the case up for years."

Ellery shrugged. "Marsh and that other law firm Benedict had wished on him wield an awful lot of clout. Well, we have to assume the holograph knocks out the earlier will and, as you said back there, whoever pulled the homicide committed a murder for nothing. This Leslie Carpenter fellow picks up all the marbles."

"You can imagine how those vultures are feeling right now. Especially the one who beat Benedict to death. . . . Something wrong, son?"

Ellery looked vague.

"You're all of a sudden a hundred miles away."

"Oh. Something's been bugging me ever since we left Johnny's bedroom."

"What's that?"

"I don't know. A feeling. That we've overlooked something."

"Overlooked what?"

Ellery braked the Cougar in the carport and switched off the ignition.

"If I could answer that, dad, I wouldn't be bugged. Out. Sack time."

Benedict's cousin Leslie drove in during the early afternoon of Monday.

To the surprise of everyone but Marsh, it was a woman who got out of the airport taxi. "It never occurred to me you'd assume the name Leslie meant a man," Marsh said to the Queens. "I've known her through Johnny since she was in deep orthodontia. How are you, Les?"

She turned a glad smile on Marsh. She was years younger than Johnny-B, and the Queens soon perceived that she was not only of a different sex from her late cousin, she was of a different species. Where Benedict had been the child of fortune, Leslie had had to scrimp all her life.

"My mother, who was Johnny's aunt—Johnny's father's sister—got the heave from my grandfather. In the good old Victorian-novel style, he disinherited her. It seems that mother was too much of a rebel and didn't have the proper reverence for capital. And worst of all she insisted on falling in love with a man who had no money and no social standing." Leslie smiled mischievously. "Poor grandfather, he couldn't understand mother, and he accused daddy to his face of being— oh, dear—a 'fortune hunter.' Dad a fortune hunter! He thought less of money than even mother did."

"You paint a filial picture," Ellery smiled.

"Thank you, sir. Dad was the typical absent-minded professor who taught in a country school at a starvation salary, tyrannized by a school board who thought anybody who had read more than two books was a dues-paying Communist. He died at the age of forty-one of cancer. Mother was sickly, had a rheumatic heart . . . if this sounds like soap opera, don't blame me, it actually happened . . . and I had to go to work to support us. That meant leaving school. It was only when mother died that I was able to go back and get my degree. In sociology. I've been working in the fields of welfare and education ever since.

"Johnny evidently nursed a guilt feeling because mother had been kicked out, so that his father inherited everything and passed it along to him. Poor old John. He kept looking us up and pressing money on us. Mother and dad would never take any. Me, I wasn't the least bit proud. I gratefully accepted John's financial help after mother passed away, or I'd never have been able to go back to college at all, I had too many debts to pay off. The way I saw it," Leslie said thoughtfully, "Johnny's making it possible for someone like me to complete her education was encouraging him to do something useful with his money instead of throwing it away on a lot of gimme girls. And if that's a rationalization, so be it." And Leslie's little chin grew half an inch.

Inspector Queen (*concealing a smile*): "Miss Carpenter, did your cousin John ever indicate to you that he was going to make you the principal beneficiary of his estate under certain circumstances?"

"Under no circumstances, never! I didn't dream he'd leave me so much as grandfather's watch. We used to argue our social and political differences—remember, Al? Al will tell you I never pulled my punches with John."

"She certainly did not," Marsh said. "Johnny took a

great deal from you, Les, more than from anybody. He
was crazy about you. Maybe in love with you."

"Oh, come, Al. I don't think he ever even liked me.
I was the bone in his throat—I kept telling him I was
the voice of his superego. As far as I was concerned,
John Levering Benedict the Three was a nonproduc-
tive, useless, all-wrapped-up-in-his-own-pleasures para-
site, and I was the only one with the nerve to tell him
so. There's so much he could have done with his
money!"

"Aren't you overlooking something?" Marsh asked
dryly. "He has done it, Les. Now."

Leslie Carpenter looked amazed. "Do you know, I'd
forgotten! That's true, isn't it? Now I can do all the
wonderful things . . . ."

There was something about the capsule autobiog-
rapher that tickled Ellery, and he surveyed her with
an interest not altogether professional. On the outside
she was a porcelain bit of femininity, looking as if you
could see through her if you held her up to the light,
but experience in reading character told him she was
made of tough materials. There was a tilt to her little
head, a glint in her eyes, that signified *Sturm und
Drang* for anyone she disapproved of.

But what he perceived in her, or thought he did, went
deeper than a strength developed through the exercise of poverty and the need to fight back in a world
that crushed pacifists. There was a womanliness in her,
a sweet underlying honesty, a lack of guile, that drew
him. (And she possessed that paradox of nature, blue
eyes that were warm.)

He thought it wonderful, then, that Leslie turned
to Marsh and asked abruptly, "How much am I inher-
iting, Al?"

"The answer to that goes back to Johnny's father.
Under Benedict Senior's will, on Johnny's death his heir
or heirs would receive the entire income from the

Benedict holdings. Mind you, Leslie, I said income,
not principal. Mr. Benedict didn't believe in distribut-
ing principal, even after he was dead. The principal
remains in trust and intact."

"Oh," Leslie said. "That sounds like a letdown. How
much will the income come to?"

"Well, you'll be able to do a few good works with
it, Les, and maybe have a few dollars left over for yourself. Let me see . . . oh, you should be collecting an
income of some three million dollars a year."

"My God!" Leslie Carpenter whispered; and she fell,
weeping, into Marsh's arms.

The press and the networks had descended in clouds
late on Sunday, when the news of Johnny-B's murder
got out of Wrightsville. The invasion brought with it
the usual orgy of sensationalism and slush. Newby and
his small department, groggy from coping with the
riotous student mass-trip at Fyfield Gunnery, had their
hands overfull; in the end, the chief had to call on the
state police for assistance, and a number of importunate
newsmen and slop sisters were escorted from the
grounds. Order was restored when a news pool was
agreed upon, consisting of one representative each of
the wire services, the TV networks, and the radio people. A single round-robin conference with the ex-wives
and Leslie Carpenter was authorized to take place in
the living room of the main house, a brouhaha that the
Queens and Newby observed out of range of the cameras, watching and listening for some slip or lapse, no
matter how tiny or remote. But if their quarry was one
of the disinherited women, she was too guarded to give
herself away. The women merely contended for cam-
era exposure and had nothing but kind and grieving
words for the passing of their Lord Bountiful. (The
trio had evidently made a pact not to malign Benedict
in public for tactical reasons, at least until they could

consult counsel about the will trick and the prestidigitation of their millions.) Leslie Carpenter limited herself to an expression of surprise at her windfall and the statement that she had "plans for the money" which she would disclose "at the proper time."

At this juncture Marcia Kemp was heard to say, "Which is going to be never, baby!"—not by the press, fortunately for her, only by the Queens and Chief Newby. They questioned the redhead about the remark later, when the news people were gone. She explained quickly that she had been referring to the coming contest over the holograph will, which she was "sure" she, Alice, and Audrey would win; she had certainly not intended the remark as a threat to Miss Carpenter. (Newby thereupon assigned an officer to keep an eye on Miss Carpenter.)

But that was the only note of discord.

There followed the surprising episode of the little hill and what stood upon it.

During the idyllic (pre-homicide) part of their stay, while exploring Benedict's property, the Queens had come across what looked like a Greek antiquity in miniature, a sort of ancient temple for dolls, with a little pediment and some more than creditable frieze-figures of a bucolic nature, little Doric columns, and for fillip two heavily stained-glass little windows. The tiny structure stood on the crest of a hillock surrounded by meadow, a pleasant if incongruous sight in the New England countryside.

The Queens, *père et fils*, walked around the diminutive construction wondering what it was. It did not look old, yet it did not look new, either. Ellery tried the adult-sized bronze door and found it as immovable as the entrance to SAC headquarters.

"A playhouse for some rich man's little girl?" the Inspector ventured at last.

"If so, it was an expensive one. This is genuine marble."

It did not occur to either man that it might have been built by John Levering Benedict III to shelter his moldering mortality.

But that was what it proved to be, a mausoleum. "Johnny left a covering letter about it," Al Marsh told them Monday night. "He wanted to be laid away in it. He had a horror of being planted in the elaborate family vaults—there's one in Seattle and one in Rhinebeck, New York. I don't really know why—in fact, I doubt Johnny did himself. At heart he was a rebel like his Aunt Olivia—Leslie's mother—only he had too much of his father in him, who in turn was dominated all his life by the grandfather. Or, as Johnny put it, 'I inherited my father's disease—no guts.' It's my opinion Johnny hated everything that had gone into creating the Benedict fortune.

"Anyway, shortly after he purchased this property he designed the mausoleum—rather, had an architect blueprint it to his specifications—and hired a couple of oldtimers, country masons, practically an extinct breed, I understand, from around here to build it on that rise above the meadow. He brought in a sculptor from Boston to do the figures in the pediment; and the only reason he went to Boston for one is that he couldn't find a local sculptor. Johnny loved this town and the surrounding country. The marble comes from the Mahoganies up there, native stuff. He left a special maintenance fund in perpetuity, by the way. He said, 'I expect to lie here for a long time.'"

"But how did he finagle a cemetery permit?" Inspector Queen asked curiously. "Doesn't this state have a law against burial in private ground?"

"I had something to do with that, Inspector. I rooted around and found that the section of land where that hill and meadow lie has been in dispute between

Wrightsville and Wright County for over a hundred
and seventy-five years, the result of a surveying error
in the eighteenth century. Wrightsville's always claimed
that the meadow is within the town limits, with Wright
County just as stubbornly maintaining that it's outside
the disputed line. The claims have never been satis-
factorily adjudicated; it's one of those Biblical problems these old communities run into sometimes, with
no Solomon around to settle them. I worked through a
local law firm, Danzig and Danzig, and we just stepped
into the legal No Man's Land and presented the con-
tending parties with the accomplished fact. The thing
is in such a tangle that I could assure Johnny he might
count on resting in peace in that miniature temple till
the day after Armageddon. So he went ahead with his
plans."

On Wednesday, Benedict's body was officially re-
leased by the coroner's office (the jury, having little of
evidential substance to go on but the meager autopsy
report, found that the deceased had come to his death
"by a homicide caused by a blunt instrument here-
under described at the hand of person or persons unknown"); and on Friday, which was the third of April,
Benedict was laid to rest in his meadow.

There had been a fierce if hushed competition for
the business. Wrightsville's mortuary needs were served
by three establishments: Duncan Funeral Parlors (the
oldest in town), the Eternal Rest Mortuary, and Twin
Hill Eternity Estates, Inc. They cuddled together on
the east side of Upper Whistling Avenue (across from
The Nutte Shop and Miss Sally's Tea Room) like three
cotyledons in a seed. The notoriety of the case, which
in an earlier day would have caused the conservative
gentry of the embalming fluid to shudder and shy,
only spurred their descendants to the chase; it was not
every day that a local undertaking parlor was called

on to bury a Benedict, and a murdered Benedict at
that.

The determinant in the selection of the Duncan es-
tablishment was free enterprise. The incumbent, Philbert Duncan, had absorbed his art at the knees of the
old master, his father, whom envious detractors had
called "the slickest people-planter east of L.A." Johnny
Benedict's letter of instructions on the subject of his
interment had directed that his remains be encased
in a stainless-steel inner container of a solid bronze
casket of specified quality and design. No such magnificent box being available at any of the Wrightsville
parlors, there was talk of postponing the funeral until
the appropriate one could be shipped up from Boston.
But Philbert Duncan drove over to Connhaven in the
middle of the night of Wednesday–Thursday (presumably after moonset by the light of a dark lantern)
and returned in triumph at dawn carting the specified
coffin; it turned out that he had a cousin, one Duncan
Duncan, who was in the business in Connhaven, a good-
sized city in which demands for $5000 caskets, while
uncommon, were not unknown.

Benedict's instructions had also called for an Epis-
copal funeral service, since he had been baptized and
confirmed in the Anglican communion; and old Father
Highmount was pressed into service for the occasion,
having to come out of retirement because his successor,
young Reverend Boyjian (he was, to Ernest Highmount's horror, not only Low Church but of *Arme-
nian* descent!) was in the Bahamas with his wife on a
vacation financed by the vestry in lieu of a much-
needed rise in salary.

As the one and only next of kin, Leslie Carpenter
decided to bypass a formal service in the church because of the rowdy press and the great curiosity of
the public. A delegation of Benedict's closest friends,
selected by Leslie on Marsh's advice, came by invita-

tion from south, east, and west. It was calculatedly not large, so that the company assembled on the meadow before the little Greek temple at two o'clock Friday afternoon, even with the pool from the news media included, was handled without difficulty by Chief Newby's officers, with the state police relegated to the boundaries of the property to balk crank crashers and just plain nosy noonans from town.

It could not be said that Father Highmount produced a snappy service. He had always been a mumbler, a failing that had hardly improved with age; he was also suffering from a sloppy spring cold and he was having trouble with his dentures, so that most of what he said before the mausoleum came out a mumbo jumbo of mutters, squeaks, snuffles, and spit. About all the Queens heard with any clarity were "resurrection and the life," "*Dominus illuminatio* The Lord is my light," "My soul fleeth," "St. John fourteen one," and a final mighty "one God, world without end Amen!" which was miraculously free of sludge.

But the day was lovely, the breeze ruffled the old man's few fine silvery hairs in benediction, and no one seemed to mind the unintelligibility of his message to the dead man. For there was a quality of sincerity in his performance, a devotion to what he was saying over the invisible stranger in the casket (Leslie had wisely decided, in view of her cousin's wounds, not to put Philbert Duncan's cosmetic artistry to the test by having an open-coffin service), even though no one understood the old man but himself—there was in this quality a something that raised the flesh and brought a meaning out of the mystery. In spite of himself, Ellery was impressed.

He found himself reflecting that the whole bit—Benedict's valueless life, his dearth of accomplishment in spite of unlimited means, his uncompensated guilts, his failure to contribute anything but money to sad and

greedy women who promptly threw it away, and finally a brutal death on the eve of what might have
turned out to be his reformation—the whole bit was out
of the theater of the absurd. Or, for that matter (thinking of the mausoleum), of Sophocles.

Still, he had redeemed part of his worthlessness.
Aside from the mysterious Laura, Benedict had thought
to provide for the far-out contingency—an act of in-
credible foresight, when one thought about it—that he
might not survive the weekend. In which case, he had
decided, everything went to little Leslie Carpenter, who
had a very positive idea—as she had apparently told
him so often to his face—of what could be done with
three million a year.

So his life had not been all wasteland.

Ellery half expected the hapless Laura to put in an
appearance at the funeral—in a dramatic black veil
surely—weeping for sympathetic cameras and perhaps
angling for a paid interview with LIFE or LOOK, or the
slushier newspapers. But no mystery woman showed
up in Wrightsville or sent a telegram or a letter to
Leslie or Marsh or the police; and no unidentified funeral wreath arrived to pique the press, Newby, or the
Queens.

Only Leslie, Marsh, a trapped Miss Smith, the three
ex-wives, Chief Newby, and the Queens remained while
Duncan's assistants carried the bronze casket into the
mausoleum, set it precisely on the catafalque, arranged the many wreaths and floral baskets artistically,
and emerged to lock the door and hand the key to
Chief Newby. Who turned it over to Marsh, as the attorney of record, for safekeeping until the estate
should be settled.

There was no conversation on the tramp back
through the fields to the house. Glancing over his
shoulder, Ellery saw the stained glass in the little building glow in the sunlight, and he hoped that Johnny

Benedict was comforted, although—his unorthodox views being what they were—he doubted it.

The fleet of taxis and private cars had all driven off; only two state policemen were left guarding the road; in spite of the sun and the breeze, there was a clammy feel to the air, and not only the women shivered.

Waiting for them inside was young Lew Chalanski, an assistant prosecutor of Wright County, the son of a popular former prosecutor, Judson Chalanski. Young Chalanski conferred with Chief Newby aside, smiled his father's famous vote-getting smile, and left.

Newby's poet's face was preoccupied.

"I understand everyone here except Alice Tierney, who's local, lives in New York City. You're all free to go home."

"Meaning you haven't got a damned thing on us," Marcia Kemp said, tossing her red head like a flamenco dancer. "Or you'd never let us out of your state."

"Correction. What it means, Miss Kemp," the chief said, "is that we haven't enough evidence against any individual to bring before a grand jury at the present time. But I want to emphasize: this is an open case, under active investigation, and you three ladies are the hot suspects. Do any of you have plans to leave New York State in the immediate future?" They said they did not. "That's fine. If that situation should change, however, get in touch first with Inspector Queen at his office in Centre Street. The Inspector's agreed to act as liaison man for us up here."

"How cosy," Audrey Weston sniffed.

"We cops stick together—sometimes," Newby said. "Well, ladies and gentlemen, that's it for now. This house, as the scene of a homicide, is going to be under seal, so I'd appreciate it if you left as soon as possible."

On the plane out of Boston the Inspector said, "Why so close-mouthed, Ellery?"

"I can't decide whether to admire the cleverness or marvel at the stupidity."

"Of whom? What are you talking about?"

"Of whoever left those three things in Johnny's bedroom along with his body. Each one points to a different ex-Mrs. Benedict."

"We've been all through that. It's a cinch somebody planted them."

"It certainly looks that way."

"The thing is, though—what would the point be of framing three different women for the murder? And aside from that. A frameup has to make sense on the face of it—it has to look legitimate if it's to fool the cops. What investigating officer in his right mind would believe that three women visited that bedroom, presumably at different times, and each one dropped an article of her clothing on the scene, presumably in her excitement or by accident, and so implicated herself? Anyone who'd expect a 'frameup' like that to work would have to be AWOL from the cuckoo house."

Ellery stared out the window at the flooring of cloud they were gliding over, and he nodded. "It's much likelier we're dealing with Miss Smarty Pants. Who lifted something belonging to the other two and deliberately left all the articles—her own included—on the scene in order to spread the inevitable suspicion and so, so to speak, distribute her guilt. She knew that she and the other two ex-wives were the natural—in fact, the only viable—suspects. Since all three had identical motive, opportunity, and access to the weapon—in effect, making herself one-third of a suspect instead of a standout individual."

"Unless it was a conspiracy," Inspector Queen mused. "The three of them, recognizing they were all in the same boat, ganging up on Benedict."

"That's the one situation in which they wouldn't

have left clues to themselves at all," Ellery retorted. "No, it was just one of them."

"But you aren't satisfied."

"Well, no," Ellery said, "I'm not."

"What's bugging you?"

"The whole thing."

The plane hummed along.

"And another thing," the Inspector said. "Why did I let you con me into promising Newby I'd follow through on this Laura woman? God knows I carry a heavy enough case load as it is! And suppose we find her—so what? I can't see how she could possibly be implicated."

"Unless Johnny told her something."

"Like what? Spell it out for an old illiterate."

"You also weren't cut out to be a comedian! She has to be found, dad, you know that, long shot or not. It shouldn't be too hard. He must certainly have been seen with her in public. Marsh can tell you Johnny's favorite haunts."

"Newby also asked me to check out the three exes," his father grumbled.

"*Noblesse oblige.* Some day Anse may be able to help you out on a tough Manhattan homicide."

"And you're the lousy comic's son," the Inspector said tartly; after which they flew in silence.

But not all the way. Because ten minutes out of Kennedy Ellery suddenly said, as if they had never stopped talking, "Of course, this is all on the assumption that Johnny was slugged by Marcia, or Audrey, or Alice. Suppose he wasn't."

"You suppose," his father retorted. "My supposer is all tired out. Who else could it have been?"

"Al Marsh."

The Inspector swerved in his seat. "Why in hell should Marsh have knocked Benedict off?"

"I don't know."

"He's independently wealthy, or if he's in financial trouble he certainly didn't stand to gain anything under Benedict's wills. He was also Benedict's personal attorney, confidant, closest friend—what earthly reason would Marsh have to splash Benedict's brains all over the place?"

"I told you, I don't know. But we do know he had the same opportunity and access to the weapon that the three women had. So all he lacks is motive to be as suspect as they are. If you're going to lend Newby a hand, dad, I suggest you dig into Marsh and see if you can come up with a possible motive. My offhand guess would be women."

"Laura?" the Inspector said instantly.

Ellery looked out the window.

"I love the way you assign the work," his father said, sinking back. "Any other little thing?"

"Yes." Ellery's nose wrinkled. "And this one makes me feel like a heel."

"No kidding. Let me in on it."

"Leslie Carpenter. It's a thousand-to-one shot, but . . . check out her alibi for last Saturday night."

And so, with the jet touching down on a runway in the Borough of—by coincidence—Queens, their vacation came to an end and one of Ellery's queerest cases began.

2.
The
Second
Life

WRIGHTSVILLE, April 9 (API)—
The nationwide search for "Laura
Doe" has turned up 48 Laura Does
who claim to be the mysteriously
missing fiancee of the late John Levering Benedict III, millionaire playboy murdered on the night of March
28–29 on his hideaway estate in New
England.

Anselm Newby, chief of police of
Wrightsville, where the crime took
place, believes that there has been a
misunderstanding on the part of the
public. "Doe is a name given by the
law to people whose last names are not
known," Chief Newby said in a statement issued today. "We do not know
the missing Laura's family name. It is
almost certainly not Doe. That would
have to be a miracle."

Sergeant Thomas Velie: Your name is?
Claimant: Laura-Lou Loverly.
Sgt. V.: Beg pardon?
Cl.: It used to be Podolsky. But it's Loverly now.
Sgt. V.: Address?
Cl.: It's that big apartment house on West 73rd and Amsterdam. I can never remember the number.
Sgt. V.: New York City.
Cl.: Where else?
Sgt. V.: Your letter claims you're the Laura that John Levering Benedict the Three promised to marry. Tell me the circumstances, Miss Podolsky.
Cl.: Loverly. Notice how close it is to Levering?
Sgt. V.: How long you been calling yourself Loverly?
Cl.: Since way before, don't worry.
Sgt. V.: Since way before when?
Cl.: Before I met this john.
Sgt. V.: Okay. The circumstances of your meeting.
Cl.: Well, this particular evening he was up in my apartment, see?
Sgt. V.: Doing what?
Cl.: What do johns usually do in a girl's apartment?
Sgt. V.: You tell me, lady.
Cl.: I don't believe I care for your tone of voice, Officer. You can't talk to me like I'm some ten-dollar trick.
Sgt. V.: How did he happen to be in your apartment?
Cl.: A girl can have relationships with people, can't she? Johnny phoned me. For like an appointment.
Sgt. V.: Did he identify himself as John Levering Benedict Three?
Cl.: Are you kidding? Who listens to names in my set?
Sgt. V.: Where did he get your phone number?
Cl.: We had mutual friends.

Sgt. V.: Like for instance.

Cl.: Oh, no. You ain't got—haven't some pigeon here. I don't drag my friends into fuzzyland.

Sgt. V.: All right. Describe this Johnny.

Cl.: Dressed?

Sgt. V.: I'm not interested in his wardrobe. I mean color of eyes, hair, height, weight, build, scars, birthmarks, and etcetera.

Cl.: To tell the truth, it's kind of hazy. With all the men-friends I got. I mean, but it was the same john, believe you me. I recognized him right off from the news photos. Look, Sarge, he was sloshed to the eyebrows that night. So he wants to know—like they do —how I got into the life. You know. So I give him the usual sob story and, so help me, he starts crying on my bozoom. "You poor, poor kid," he says, "what a lousy bitch of a break. You deserve better. Every girl does. So you know what, Laura-Lou? I'm going to marry you." Just like that, so help me. Of course, I didn't take him serious, you understand. Not until I read—

Sgt. V.: Date.

Cl.: What?

Sgt. V.: What date did this proposal of marriage happen on?

Cl.: I jotted it down in my little book somewhere. Here. See? March 22nd.

Sgt. V.: No, I can't touch it. Refer to it if you have to. Was that March 22nd of this year, Miss Podolsky— I mean, Loverly?

Cl.: Sure this year.

Sgt. V.: Thank you. Don't call us, we'll call you.

Cl.: You giving me the brush? Just like that? What are you, a fuzz wisenheimer?

Sgt. V.: One more lying peep out of you, sister, and I'll book you for wasting a city employe's time. On

March twenty-two Mr. Benedict was in London, England. That way out.

Vincentine Astor? She don't work here no more. Just didn't show one night, and not even a postal card since. That's the way most of these broads are, you can't depend on them worth a damn. The best ones are the marrieds who are supporting some bum and a couple kids, they can't afford to walk out on the management. Why she quit? How do I know why? Who knows why they do anything? Maybe she didn't like the color of the hatcheck room. No, I don't remember him. Not from this photo, anyways. Sure I've seen other pictures of him in the papers, TV, you don't have to get sore. I know they say he came into my club a few times, I'm not saying he didn't. I'm only saying I don't remember seeing him. Kickbacks to the what? Oh, the mob. What are you talking about? I don't know what you're talking about. Oh, you mean Vincentine might have been kicking back some of her pay to some hoods or something and fell behind and got in dutch? Look, I run a clean club here, Officer, I don't know nothing about no mob. What? When didn't she show up? You mean when did Vincentine rat on me? Wait a minute while I look it up. Yeah, here. She quit me it was Sunday, March twenty-ninth. Yeah, yeah, her home address. Here. Say, Officer, you wouldn't happen to know of a stacked broad wants a job? Reliable? You know?

No, Miss Astor moved out the end of the month, let's see now, yeah, as of the thirty-first it was. Yes, sir, paid up right to the day she left. No, these are furnished, so she didn't have to call a mover or anything, just packed her bags and called a cab. No, I don't know a thing about her private life. I don't stick my nose in my roomers' keyholes like some landladies around here I could mention. As long as they're quiet, I always say. And don't give my house a bad name. What man? Oh. No, sir, can't say I ever did. I mean, I never saw him in this house. Though his picture does look sort of familiar, you might say. Say, isn't this the playboy who—? Well, I never. I'll be. No, she didn't leave no forwarding address; I asked her for one but she said it's not necessary, I won't be getting any mail. Was that girl mixed up with *him*?

Excerpt Interview, N.Y.P.D.:

Detective Piggott: Name, Madam?
Claimant: Miss.
Det. P.: Miss what?
Cl.: Laura De Puyster Van Der Kuyper.
Det. P.: Hold it. Are they like one word, or—?
Cl.: De—Puyster—Van—Der—Kuyper. P-u-y. K-u-y.
Det. P.: Yes, ma'am. Address?
Cl.: Definitely not.
Det. P.: Pardon?
Cl.: I do not have to tell you my place of residence. I never give that information to anyone. A girl never knows.
Det. P.: Miss Kuyper—
Cl.: Miss Van Der Kuyper.
Det. P.: Miss Van Der Kuyper I have to put your address down on this report. It's regulations.
Cl.: Not my regulations. You claim you're a police officer—
Det. P.: What else would I be? Sitting here at this table in police headquarters asking you questions?
Cl.: I've heard of that kind of smooth talk before. It's the way they get into your apartment and attack you.
Det. P.: If you were attacked, Miss Van Der Kuyper, that's a different department.
Cl.: I'm not going to tell you about it. Or anyone.

You'd like me to, wouldn't you? Splash me all over the filthy newspapers.

Det. P.: Age?

Cl.: You may put down I am over twenty-one.

Det. P. (begins to speak, changes his mind, writes, "Over 50"): Look, Miss Van Der Kuyper, we have this confidential communication from your claiming you know or rather knew John L. Benedict Third and you are the Laura he allegedly proposed marriage to. Is that correct?

Cl.: That is precisely correct.

Det. P.: Now. How long were you acquainted with this John L. Benedict Third?

Cl.: For ages and eons. Veritably.

Det. P.: Could you be like more exact, Miss Van Der Kuyper?

Cl.: Exact about what?

Det. P.: About the time you made his acquaintance.

Cl.: Is there time in Paradise? Our marriage plans were murmured in Heaven. I am not ashamed to proclaim our affection to the universe. We met in a secret Persian garden.

Det. P.: Where, where?

Cl.: It is so crystal in my memory. That soft, immoral—immortal evening. The moon great as with child. The drunken scent of frangipani sweet in our quivering nostrils, and of divine cinnamon, and anise, and thyme.

Det. P.: Yes, ma'am. This secret garden was in Persia, you say? Just where in Persia?

Cl.: Persia?

Det. P.: I should think that does it, Miss Van Der Kuyper. Fine, fine, it's okay. You'll hear from us in due course. No, ma'am, that's our job. If you'll kindly follow the matron . . . .

Trip sheets for when did you say? Tuesday, March

thirty-first. Wait a minute. Hey, Schlockie, I got to talk
to you; look, Officer, if you'll give me a few seconds.
We got nothing but kooks roll out of this shop.

Oh, say, you still checking the air pollution in here?
I'm sorry, Officer, you can't take his life if you don't
make a funny once in a while, excuse me. These hackies
are going to be my death, to listen to them they got
beefs not even the Mayor heard of. Yeah, certainly.
Tuesday, March three-one. Here it is, Joseph Levine.
You want his license number? Picked up the fare at
that address as of ten thirty-four A.M., discharged pas-
senger at Grand Central. No, Joe won't be pulling in
till four forty-five, five this afternoon. Think nothing
of it. Always glad to do the P.D. a favor. Yeah.

> Finally, there's the story out of Wash-
> ington, where rumors grow thicker
> than cherry blossoms at Japanese festi-
> val time, that a subcommittee of Con-
> gress may launch an investigation into
> the search for the mysterious Laura in
> the John Benedict murder case, on the
> alleged ground that there is no Laura
> and never has been, that it's all been
> some sort of press agent's plot to pro-
> mote something or other, a movie or a
> new TV series or something, as such
> constituting a fraud on the public in-
> nocence, and therefore being the le-
> gitimate concern of the nation's
> lawmakers, who clearly have nothing
> more important to do. Good night,
> Chuck.

My dear fellow, I knew Johnny-B as well as any man
alive—even though Al Marsh didn't have the elemental
good manners to invite me to the obsequies—and I
swear to you on my honor, and you may print this,
that when Johnny wrote that clause in his will about

some "Laura" or other and how he was going to marry her, he was simply pulling the leg of the whole mother-frugging world. He told me in absolute confidence that he was through with the marriage bit. It was just after his final decree from that country R.N. from—what's it called? Titusville? Dwightsville? something rare and wonderful like that. "Muzzie," Johnny said to me, "just between you, me, and the nearest pub I've had it. Up to here. No more wedding marches for Johnny-B. From now on I'm strictly tone-deaf, fancy-free, and staying away from aisles." His exact words. And you may quote me. No, not Mussie. Muzzie, with a double z.

> The jet set continues in a busy-buzzy-tiz over the Johnny Benedict tragedy. There has been hardly any other topic of conversation among the B.P. for weeks and weeks, or at least it seems weeks and weeks. Everyone wants to know who Laura is—Laura, now known among Johnny-B's cronies as "the last woman in his life." Compounding the mystery is the fact that no one can recall anyone named Laura in or out of Johnny's circle. . . . This column can now reveal that Jackie and Ari . . . .

Yeah, I'm Levine. Joseph W. What fare? Now, how the hell do you expect me to remember some dame I picked up God knows how far back? I know, I know, I can read the date on the trip sheet. Okay, so she was a big platinum-type broad with a built. You got any idea how many dames like that a New York hackie picks up in a day? Look, Mac, I'd like to help you out but I just ain't with it on a hooha like this. I hack I figure three out of every ten fares to some terminal, and what I do at Grand Central is I dump them at the bottom of the ramp, pick up another fare, and away I go. If they start telling me the story of their lives and why they're leaving New York and where they're going I blow my ears out like a whale or something and I let it go right on through—I should worry why they're leaving and where they're off to? Sorry, Officer, I'm such a drip-dry on this. Let me tell you in confidence, though, I don't think there's *enough* police brutality. Some of the creeps I run into in my line of work you couldn't beat their brains out with a stainless-steel jack handle, they ain't got any. Thanks? For what? Did I tell you something?

Look, Sidney, we're supposed to be keeping our mouths shut about the Benedict case—orders straight from Inspector Queen. I know I owe you. Okay, but for chrissake protect your source. We just put out a flyer on this Vincentine Astor. No, we haven't got a thing on her. Except what's likely a coincidence that she quit her job at the Boy-Girl Club March twenty-ninth. No, I'm telling you, Vincentine isn't wanted except for routine questioning. We have no hard evidence that Benedict ever knew her except to check his hat with. Yeah, we know he visited the Boy-Girl Club a number of times within the past few months. If Vincentine was the hatcheck girl Benedict was giving the rush to lately, he sure changed his M.O., because he must have met her strictly on the q.t. away from his regular hangouts. The general feeling around here is that the reason she quit at the club and left town two days later had not a damn thing to do with Benedict. I'll give you a little bonus, Sidney, and then I got to go. The word is that the brass upstairs are sore as hell at Inspector Queen for getting New York mixed up in this Benedict brawl, I mean to the extent of carrying the ball for this jerk-town police chief. As if we haven't got enough headaches around here. Who? No, I haven't seen Ellery for days. I guess he heard the rumor, too, and doesn't want to get his old man in worse dutch than he is already.

MEMORANDUM

TO: Inspector Richard Queen, N.Y.P.D.
FROM: Anselm Newby, Chief, Wrightsville

I wish I could report progress of some sort. I can't. The only fingerprints we found in Benedict's bedroom were his, Morris Hunker's, and Annie Findlay's, and Morris's and Annie's had perfectly good reasons to be there. The stains on Benedict's robe and pajamas and in the room generally are all of the same blood-type as his. The iron of the weapon is a rough welding job and would normally take poor prints, our tech man says, but he has reason to believe that it was also wiped clean with something just in case. He was not able to bring out so much as a partial latent. We have not been able to come up with a lead to any suspicious person or persons in the vicinity of the Benedict property on the night of the murder. The detailed p.m. reports no additions to the prelim report. Death was definitely caused by the blows to the head, and there was no sign of toxic or other foreign substances in the internal organs except traces of alcohol accounted for by the drinks Benedict is reported to have drunk during the evening before he went to bed. And that's about it. I hope you're having better luck at your end.

Anselm Newby,
Chief of Police

P.S.: Have you had any success tracing Laura? What does Ellery say? I haven't heard a word from him since you both left Wrightsville.

A.N.

Enc.: Photocopies of fingerprint, bloodstain analysis, and autopsy reports.

MEMORANDUM

TO: Chief A. Newby, Wrightsville
FROM: R. Queen, Inspector, N.Y.P.D.

I am sorry to report that the Laura investigation is at a standstill.

We will keep at it, but of course you understand that we carry a very heavy load of our own these days which of course has to take priority over courtesy cases such as our current assistance with the Wrightsville murder.

Ellery has said very little to me about the case. My feeling is he is as hung up on it as the rest of us.

R. Queen,
Inspector, N.Y.P.D.

MEMORANDUM

TO: Inspector Richard Queen, N.Y.P.D.
FROM: Anselm Newby, Chief of Police, Wrightsville,——

I understand your position about the Benedict case, and I am sorry that your vacation in Wrightsville got you and your son involved in it. In all fairness that was none of my doing, and if my recollection is correct the original suggestion that the N.Y.P.D. help us out on the case came from Ellery.

If your case load is too heavy to enable you to assist a fellow police officer in the investigation of a prominent Manhattan multimillionaire international playboy, let me know by return mail and I will personally write to your immediate superior and take you and the N.Y.P.D. off the hook.

In the above case I should appreciate your sending me all reports you have accumulated thus far, the originals if possible, photocopies if not, especially reports concerning Audrey Weston, Marcia Kemp, and Al Marsh.

I am very grateful for your assistance.

A. Newby,
Chief, Wrightsville P.D.

TO: Chief Anselm Newby, Wrightsville Police Department
FROM: R. Queen, Inspector, N.Y.P.D.

I did not intend anything in my last note to give you the impression that I was trying to go back on my promise. I was merely pointing out that we could not afford to put as much time, effort, and man-hours into an out-of-city (and state) case as if the homicide was within the N.Y.P.D.'s direct jurisdiction.

I have shown your memorandum to my superiors and they have agreed to allow me and my staff to continue assisting you in the Benedict investigation, especially since—as I pointed out in a conference just concluded with certain high officers of the Department —ramifications of the case lead directly into New York City and two of the three prime suspects are residents of Manhattan.

As a routine matter we have checked out Leslie Carpenter's whereabouts on the night of Saturday–Sunday, March 28–29. She has an airtight alibi for the general time-period of the crime. She was in Washington, D.C., from late afternoon of Friday, March 27, to the evening of Sunday, March 29, attending a two-day Urban Corps conference. Every hour of Miss Carpenter's time during those two days is accounted for.

There is nothing further to report on Audrey Weston and Marcia Kemp. Both are keeping pretty much to their Manhattan apartments. If they have seen an attorney about the will situation we do not have any information. I assume there is similarly nothing from your end on Alice Tierney.

I will soon be sending you a background report on Al Marsh, per your request. Best personal regards.

Richard Queen,
Inspector, N.Y.P.D.

"On Marsh?" Ellery said, reaching across the Inspector's desk.

Inspector Queen ignored the hand. "You can look at it later. There's nothing in it you don't know about him except you never mentioned that Al isn't his real name."

"I never mentioned it because, if you were a friend of Al's in our Harvard days, you were quickly conditioned not to. I suppose the report notes that he was christened Aubrey, as in C. Aubrey Smith, rest his stiff-upper soul. Anyone who called Al Aubrey like as not wound up with a shiner or a bloody nose."

"According to one source," the Inspector said, "'Aubrey' was an inspiration of his mama's. I can't say I blame him. It's a hell of a tag for a grown man to have to tote around."

"Al once told me that when he was in grammar and prep school—private, of course, about which he was surprisingly bitter—he had to lick every kid in his grade before he made the 'Al' stick. 'Al' doesn't stand for Albert, or Alfred, or Aloysius, by the way—for just Al, period."

"His fancy ancestors must be swinging in their graves."

"By the time he got to Harvard he was too big to tackle even in fun. He was a varsity back and he won the Ivy League wrestling title in his weight class. I doubt if anybody in the Yard knew his name was Aubrey except his most intimate pals, and we had more sense than to bring it up. But I never did learn much about his family background. Al didn't talk about it."

The Inspector scanned the report. "His father came from a line of international bankers and high society. His mother, it says here, was a Rushington, whatever that is. Marsh Senior was killed in the crash of his private plane just after Al was born."

"That might explain something," Ellery said. "He used to talk about his mother all the time. Never about his father."

"Mrs. Marsh never remarried, even though she was a young woman when her husband died. She devoted the rest of her active life to Aubrey, and when she became an invalid he returned the service—looked after her like a nurse. The feeling among his friends is that that's why he never got married. And by the time his mother kicked off he was a confirmed bachelor."

"His mother left everything to him, of course."

"What else?"

"How much?"

"Loads. Marsh isn't as rich as Benedict was, but after the first few millions is there any difference?"

"Then Al is rock-solid financially."

"Like the Chase National Bank."

"No trouble? Gambling, bad investments, anything like that?"

"No. He's pretty much a conservative where money is concerned. He doesn't gamble at all."

"So there's no motive."

"Not a whimper. He doesn't gain from any of Benedict's wills, he wouldn't need it if he did, and every source we've tapped indicates that he's a topflight attorney with a reputation for absolute personal honesty as well as professional competence."

But Ellery persisted. "That kind of conclusion depends on the reliability of the source. Have you been able to investigate his handling of Johnny's affairs?"

"Yes, and as far as we can tell it's all legal and aboveboard. Granted we couldn't be sure without a plant inside, what could Marsh hope to accomplish by diddling with Benedict's funds? It could only be for a financial reason, and we're absolutely positive Marsh has no money worries whatsoever. Anyway, most of Benedict's capital is under the management of Brown, Brown, Mattawan, Brown, and Loring, that old-line law firm, and not under Marsh's at all."

"How about women?"

"How about them?"

"I mean a possible romantic rivalry."

"Nothing. What we've dug out indicates that Marsh has never been involved with any number on Benedict's hit parade except, on occasion, in his legal capacity, when Benedict wanted to pay some girl off or make some sort of settlement on her to close the book when he'd got tired of her."

"And the ex-wives?"

Inspector Queen shook his head. "Nothing there, either. Marsh got to know them through Benedict, except the Kemp girl, and his contacts with them were strictly as Benedict's friend and, in the course of time, as Benedict's attorney. Anyway, Marsh's preference in women is the opposite of Benedict's. Marsh goes for small, feminine-type females."

Ellery grinned. "Al once showed me a photo of his mother. She was a small, feminine-type female."

His father frowned. "Will you clear out of my office and let me do some of my own work?" The Inspector had an old-fashioned sense of propriety, and cracks about possibly unhealthy mother-son relationships did not amuse him. As Ellery was opening the door the old man asked, "Where you off to now?"

"I thought of something I want to ask Al about Johnny. I'll tell you about it later."

Mr. Marsh, Miss Smith said, was tied up with a client and could not under any circumstances be disturbed. Anyway, Mr. Marsh never saw anyone except by appointment. Unless, her hostile glance suggested, it was the kind of snoop business that experience had taught her to associate with the presence of one Ellery Queen? Miss Smith's tone and demeanor were such that, had she been barefoot, love-beaded, and unkempt, she would have spat the word "pig" at him, with an appropriate modifying obscenity; as it was, being a lady and the product of a no doubt Victorian mother, she could only resort to the subtleties of eye- and vocal cord-play to express her loathing.

Mr. Queen, ever the gentleman in the presence of a lady, scribbled a few words and asked with utter *politesse* that Miss Smith in her secretarial capacity convey the note to Mr. Marsh, client notwithstanding.

Miss Smith: I can't do that.

Mr. Queen: You astonish me, Miss Smith. It may be that you will not do that, or that you may not do that, but that you cannot do it—since you seem normally ambulatory and otherwise in unimpaired possession of your physical faculties—I do not for an instant believe.

Miss Smith: How you do go on. You think you're smart. You're the kind who makes fun of people.

Mr. Queen: I'm emphatically nothing of the sort. I simply feel it my duty to the cause of semantic hygiene never to allow a grammatical slovenliness to go uncleansed.

Miss Smith: You must have a real dandy time all by yourself listening to the radio and TV commercials pollute the English language.

Mr. Queen: Miss Smith, how marvelous! You have a sense of humor! Now will you take that note in to Al, like I asked you?

Miss Smith: You made a booboo! You said 'like' instead of 'as'!

Mr. Queen: Alas, so I did. Demonstrating the fallibility of even the purest purist. The note, Miss Smith?

Miss Smith: You made that mistake purposely. You're pulling my leg.

Mr. Queen: No, but is it permitted? I might add that I have admired your limbs, Miss Smith, from the moment I laid eyes on them. Ah, you're smiling. We advance. The note?

Al Marsh came out for a moment, glancing at Miss Smith in a puzzled way.

"Miss Smith seems all of a flutter, Ellery. Charm, or an emergency?"

"Hardly the first, and no to the second. It's just that I wanted to ask you something about Johnny. It won't take a minute—"

"I don't have a minute. The old gent in my office takes a dim enough view of me as it is. His point is that keeping a man of his age waiting—he's ninety—constitutes a felonious act. How about meeting me at my place? Sevenish? Dinner, if you've no other plans. Louis used to cook at Le Pavillon. Miss Smith will give you my address if you don't know it."

It proved to be a duplex penthouse high over Sutton Place. Above the dismal city—in spite of calendars, not quite out of winter, not fully into spring—Ellery found himself luxuriating. A houseman named Estéban ushered him into a man's huge habitat of feudal oak, Spanish iron, velvets, brass, copper; a place of lofty ceilings, hunter's trophies, and weapons. While he waited for Marsh to appear Ellery strolled about taking his peculiar inventory, totting up the stock that declared the man.

There was not a trace of modernism about the apartment, such of it as he could see; it might have come out of an exclusive men's club of the Nineties. The small private gymnasium off the living room (the door was open) displayed weights, barbells, exercycles, parallel bars, a punching bag setup, and other paraphernalia of the aging ex-athlete; that was to be expected of Marlboro Man. But there were surprises.

Half a short wall was taken up with stereophonic equipment for the high fidelity reproduction of a large collection of LPs and cassettes. There was a great deal of Tchaikovsky and Beethoven, he noted, struck by the romanticism he had not associated with Marsh. The hi-fi was playing "Prince Gremin's Air" from *Eugen Onegin;* Ellery recognized the Russian-singing basso as Chaliapin, whose great masculine voice he often sought for his own reassurance.

A leaded-glass bookstack enchanted him. It contained rare American, French, and British editions of Melville, Rimbaud, Verlaine, Henry James, Proust, Wilde, Walt Whitman, Gide, and Christopher Marlowe, among many others—rank on rank of literary giants, many in first editions the sight of which made Ellery's wallet itch. There were rare art books of enormous size illustrated with the paintings and sculptures chiefly of da Vinci and Michelangelo. A row of niches in the oak walls held busts of historical figures whom Marsh evidently admired—Socrates, Plato, Alexander, Julius Caesar, Virgil, Horace, Catullus, Frederick the Great, Lord Kitchener, Lawrence of Arabia, and Wilhelm von Humboldt.

"I see you're casing my treasury," Marsh said, turning off the stereo. "Sorry to keep you waiting, but that old fellow has had me hopping all afternoon. Drink?" He had changed to a lounge suit with an open silk shirt; he wore huaraches.

"Anything but bourbon."

"You don't go for our native elixir?"

"I once got myself beastly drunk on it. Why do I malign the beasts? Humanly. I haven't been able to sniff it since."

Marsh went behind his taproom-sized bar and began with energy to make like a bartender. "You? Got drunk?"

"You make it sound like a capital crime. I'd just been extinguished by the then light of my life."

"*You?* Had an affair with a girl?"

"It certainly wasn't with a man. What do you take me for, Al?"

"Well, I don't know. Here's your gin on the rocks. That's as far from bourbon and branch as you can get." Marsh sank into a chair that dwarfed him, nuzzling a concoction of unguessable ingredients. "I've never thought of you as really human, Ellery. I must say I'm relieved."

"Thank you," Ellery said. "I envy you those first editions. I'm beginning to grasp the full advantages of wealth."

"Amen," Marsh said. "But you didn't drop into my

office this afternoon, or here tonight, to admire my etchings. What's on your mind?"

"Do you recall that Saturday night in Wrightsville, Al?"

"It's written in acid."

"As you know, I was eavesdropping from the terrace while Johnny was delivering that spiel about his new-will intentions."

"Yes?"

"Something I overheard him say that night has been bothering me. I'm not clear about what he meant. He remarked that his three marriages had been 'strictly business.' Just what did he mean by that?"

Marsh settled back with his glass and a menthol cigaret. "By the terms of his father's will, contrary to popular belief, the Benedict fortune was left in trust and all Johnny received was three hundred thousand dollars per annum out of the income from the estate. Well, I don't have to tell you that to a lad of Johnny's tastes, upbringing, and habits three hundred thousand a year didn't begin to provide for his standard of living."

"He broke his father's will?"

"Unbreakable. But not unshakable." Marsh shrugged. "Johnny asked me what, if anything, could be done to raise the ante. I studied Benedict Senior's will and found what looked like a possible loophole. More in jest than anything else I pointed it out to Johnny—a looseness of expression in one of the provisions that might yield an interpretation Mr. Benedict had never intended."

"Sounds fascinating. What was it?"

"One clause in the will gave Johnny the sum of five million dollars out of the principal estate quote 'when my son John marries' unquote."

Ellery laughed.

"Of course you'd see it. Johnny certainly did. 'When my son John marries' could reasonably be construed to mean '*whenever* my son John marries'—in other words, *every time* he married he was entitled to collect another five million from the estate. I actually wasn't serious when I called the wording of the clause to Johnny's attention, and I didn't dream he would rearrange his life to revolve around it. But that's just what he did. He insisted on going into court with our argument about construing the 'when' as 'whenever,' and it was typical Johnny-B luck that the court upheld our interpretation. So then he launched his series of marriages, divorces, and remarriages."

Ellery was shaking his head. "'Strictly business' is right. His marriages were keys to the strongbox. Another key, another haul."

"Exactly. There was no misrepresentation to the women. They understood just why he was marrying them and just what they could expect to get out of it. I might add, Ellery, that I was completely against Johnny's change of heart about those million-dollar settlements." Marsh's big hand tightened about his glass. "I suppose it's silly of me to admit this, but the fact is I had a considerable row with Johnny about that intention of his to change from the million to the hundred-thousand-dollar settlements. I told him it would be an act of bad faith, a cop-out, really, certainly unethical, and I wanted no part in it. In the end we left it unresolved—I mean my participation in it."

"When did this row take place?"

"On the jet coming back from England, when he first broached his plan."

"You sounded pretty much on Johnny's side that night, Al. Are you sure you aren't trying to snow me?"

"I'm not snowing you. Johnny made it clear to me that last weekend in Wrightsville that, friends or no friends, if I didn't do it for him he'd get some other lawyer to. It forced me to do some weighing and balancing. I'd known Johnny since we were teenagers—hell,

I loved the guy. And I could hardly defend the ethical conduct of three girls who'd walked into a cold-blooded money deal under the guise of romance with their eyes wide open. In the end I picked Johnny, as of course he knew I would. Although I confess I've had qualms since."

Ellery sipped his gin. Marsh rose to freshen his drink, whatever it was.

"All right," Ellery said at last. "I suppose it's easy to make value judgments in a vacuum. About this Laura everybody's looking for, Al. You really have no notion who she might be?"

"No. I've begun to think—along with a great many others, I understand—that Laura existed only in Johnny's fertile mind. Although what motive he could have had for writing an imaginary beneficiary into a will is beyond me."

"She exists, Al. One other thing. What was the state of Johnny's financial health around the time of his death?"

"He was ailing again. You know, Johnny was the world's softest touch. He was a lifelong victim of his guilt for having come into so much money. He especially couldn't turn down a friend. One of his last exploits—which is typical—was to build a catsup factory in Maryland somewhere to produce a new kind of goo for an old pal, so-called, whose wife came up with the recipe one night—you won't believe this—in a dream. Johnny tasted it, pronounced it divine, and before he—and it—were through he sank eight hundred thousand in it, an almost total loss. Do you want a few hundred cases? We couldn't sell any, and the last I heard Johnny was giving it away, with few takers."

"I meant, Al, was he due for another five-million-dollar marriage deal? Could that have been his reason for intending to make this Laura number four?"

"Well, according to his own words he was going to

remarry," Marsh said dryly, "and he certainly could use the five million. Draw your own conclusion."

"Then you believe that all that talk of his about the Laura romance being the real thing at last was a lot of self-deluding nonsense?"

Marsh shrugged again. "I wish I knew. It's conceivable that he may have thought he was in love for the first time in his life—for all his knocking about Johnny in some ways was still an adolescent. Yes, Estéban?"

"Louis say you and guest come now," Estéban said in considerable agitation. "Louis say you and guest no come now, he quit."

"My God." Marsh jumped to his feet, looking stricken. "Ellery, *vite, vite!*"

Louis's dinner warranted Marsh's haste. It opened with an Icre Negre caviar from Romania and a Stolichnaya vodka; the soup was a *petite marmite*, served with an 1868 Malmsey Madeira. Then Estéban brought a heavenly *quenelles* with *sauce Nantua* accompanied by an estate-bottled Montrachet, Marquis de Laguiche 1966; for the *pièce* Louis had prepared a delectable *noisettes de veau sautées*, each serving crowned with a blackish, toothsome *cèpe* which could only have come from a French boletus bed (the small round veal steaks, Ellery learned, had been flown in from Paris; the proper cut, according to the word as transmitted from Louis, was unobtainable in the United States and, even assuming it could be procured locally somewhere, Louis turned his culinary thumb down in advance. "He has nothing but contempt for the chefs in *les États-Unis*," Marsh explained, "who substitute loin or kidney veal chops for the *noisettes véritables* and call them the real thing. In fact, Louis has nothing but contempt for practically everything not French." "Forgive him, Al," Ellery pleaded, "for at least at the range your paragon of *les pots et pans* knoweth precisely what he doeth"); with the *noisettes* came, in magnificent simplicity, garnished new potatoes, a Château Haut Brion of the 1949 vintage, and a braised Romaine salad; followed by a delicate *fromage de Brie* (airmailed by Fauchon) and a Château Cheval Blanc St. Emilion 1949; a Dobos Torta which decided Ellery to make Bucharest his next continental port of call; a champagne sherbet; and finally an espresso with a thirty-year-old private-stock Monnet cognac.

"This has been one of Louis's lighter dinners, whipped up more or less on the spur," Marsh said slyly. "Nevertheless, *agréable au goût, non?*"

Ellery whispered, "*Vive la France!*"

"It's a question of professional pride, I guess," Chief Newby grumbled, leaning back in his swivel chair and tonguing a fresh cigar. "Have one?"

"I'm not smoking this week," Ellery said. "What is?"

"I've never had a homicide this important. I'd hate to flub it."

"I know what you mean."

"You don't know what I mean, Ellery. You've got too blame good a statistical record. But I'm a back-country cop who all of a sudden gets hit with a big-time case, and it's got me uptight, like the kids say. You know, I've been thinking."

"You have company, Anse. What exactly about in your case?"

"We've been going on the assumption that the motive for Benedict's killing ties in to the will situation and the three ex-wives."

"Yes?"

"Maybe no."

"Anse," Ellery said severely, "I don't appreciate anyone's cryptic remarks except my own."

"I mean, suppose the motive had nothing to do with Benedict's wills?"

"All right. For instance?"

"I don't know."

"Thank you, Chief Newby. You have now joined a very select group."

"No kid, there could be something."

"Of course, but what?"

"You haven't struck anything in New York?"

"We haven't struck anything anywhere. Dad's people have failed to turn up anything or anyone in Johnny's life that provides a possible reason for someone to break into his Wrightsville house and kill him. And by the way, Anse, did your tech men find any trace—any at all—of a B. and E.?"

"No. It was either an inside job, like we've been figuring, or an outsider who got in and out without leaving a trace. Go on, Ellery."

"Go on where? I've just completed my statement. Nobody. Not even a theory about anyone. For a while we fumbled around with a Vegas contract theory, possibly tied in somehow to Marcia Kemp—those boys hit on contract with no respect for caste or class, true democracy in action. Although the whole trend in their set these days is away from violence. But we drew a blank. No evidence that Johnny-B ever welshed on a betting loss, in Vegas or anywhere else for that matter, according to—believe me, Anse—highly reliable sources. We've turned up no involvement with the Corporation, or the Combine, or whatever the Mafia's calling itself this month. Anyway, the pro touch is missing in this murder. Contract killers come equipped with their own working tools; they certainly don't depend on picking up a Three Monkeys on the scene to beat their victim's brains out."

"Then it could have been an amateur job for a personal reason, like somebody had a grudge against him for something."

"I told you, Anse. Nothing like that has turned up."

"That doesn't mean it couldn't be."

Ellery shrugged. "I have long had a convenient murderer for cases that stall. I call him, as I pull him out of my hat, The Man From Missing Forks, Iowa. Sure it could be, Anse. Anything *could* be. But you know and I know that most homicides are committed not out of the blue for obscure or bizarre reasons by the pop-up gent from Missing Forks, but by someone connected directly or obliquely to the victim for a reason that, to the killer at least, seems perfectly sensible, if not inevitable. The problem is to put your finger on him and/or it. So far we've been surveying the terrain for all the possibles, with no luck. What you do is, you keep plugging away with the hope that sooner or later, preferably sooner, your luck is going to change."

"So it still may come down to those three women and the will," Newby grunted, emerging from his cloud.

"You don't sound satisfied."

"With that theory? It's too—now don't laugh, Ellery! —too damned easy."

"Who's laughing?"

"You sure you didn't run up here on something you're keeping back from me?"

"Anse," Ellery said, and rose. "May I have the key now?"

"Then why do you want to go back to Benedict's place?"

"You're not the only one with uneasy feelings. The key, Anse?"

"If you don't mind," the chief said, rising also, "I think I'll keep you company."

Newby drove Ellery over to the Benedict property in his 1967 unmarked Dodge (to avoid notice, he claimed); he unlocked the front door and waved Ellery in before him, following on the visitor's heels. Ellery galloped upstairs and into Johnny-B's bedroom as if he expected to be greeted there by a miracle, or the answer, which his whole air announced would have been the same thing.

"You act like you forgot something, Ellery," the Wrightsville police chief said. "What?"

"I wish I could tell you." He was looking about the room as if he had never laid eyes on it.

"You mean you won't tell me?" Newby cried.

"I mean I don't know."

"Damn it, stop answering me in riddles!" the exasperated man said. "You remind me of that Sam Lloyd puzzle book my mama used to keep in her parlor."

"I'm not being coy, Anse. I really don't know. It's simply a feeling, like yours that the three women and the will as an answer is too easy."

"But what kind of a feeling is it?"

"I've had it before," Ellery said slowly, touring the room. "Often on a case, in fact." He avoided the chalked outline of Benedict's body on the floor. "A feeling that I've missed something."

"Missed something?" Newby swung about suddenly as if he had heard a door creak open. "What?"

"That," Ellery intoned, "is the question. What? I've keel-hauled my brain, couldn't come up with it, and decided that a return to the scene might be what the doctor ordered." He paused at the bed. "Here?" Glanced at the nightstand. "There?" Into the clothes closet. "There?" At the windows. Into the bathroom.

"You're putting me on," Newby muttered. "By God, you've got me creepier than a kid in a haunted house!"

"I wish it were that ordinary," Ellery said with a sigh. "No, Anse, it's not a put-on, it's a hangup. There's something here, something I saw—something I'm seeing, damn it all!—and for the life of me I can't latch onto it." He addressed the chalk outline on the floor. "Well, it was a long shot, Johnny, and like most long shots it didn't come in." He nodded disgustedly at Newby. "I'm through here, Anse, if you are."

The first break in the case came, as breaks usually do, out of the drudgery of plodding police work.

The concentration of effort on the part of Inspector Queen's staff had been on the three ex-wives, notwithstanding Chief Newby's failure of enthusiasm. Several interesting reports on the women noted that, with the cutoff on Benedict's death of their $1000 weekly incomes, and with their cash settlements held up if not gone forever by the holograph will, two of them at least were in financial difficulties. Audrey Weston and Marcia Kemp had been living up to their alimony incomes. (Alice Tierney, Newby reported, had on the contrary been living frugally in frugal Wrightsville and had saved a considerable sum, although the settlement outlook had turned her sullen and uncommunicative.) In fact, both the blonde and the redhead had been compelled to go back to work, if any. The Weston girl was making the rounds off-Broadway, so far without success; the ex-Vegas chorine was hawking the Manhattan nightclubs through her agent for a "starring" turn somewhere. But no one was snapping up the Kemp girl, either. Apparently times had changed. The notoriety they had been enjoying as a result of the Wrightsville murder was no longer the kind of open-sesame that used to break down golden doors in the days of the New York *Mirror*.

The discovery about Marcia Kemp turned up during the routine investigation of her present and past, and the development appeared significant.

Ellery learned about it on Sunday, April 19. On arising that morning he had found himself alone in the Queen apartment, and a note from his father saying that the Inspector had had to go down to Centre Street and suggesting that Ellery follow. Which he did so precipitously that he did not even stop for his cherished Sunday breakfast of Nova Scotia salmon, sweet butter and cream cheese, *cum* generous slice of sweet Spanish onion, all on toasted bagel and accompanied by freshly brewed coffee in copious quantity.

He found Sergeant Velie with the Inspector.

"Tell him, Velie," the Inspector said.

"I think we got something, Maestro," the very large sergeant said. "Ever hear of Bernie Faulks?"

"No."

"He's a punk in the rackets, a small wheel the pigeons call The Fox, or Foxy, because he's got a genius for beating the rap. He's been collared I don't know how many times on charges that didn't stick—armed robbery, B. and E., A.D.W., burglary, you name it; his one big rap, a charge of murder during an attempted felony—armed holdup—he beat when he was acquitted through the failure of a key witness to come through for the D.A. This *shtunk* Faulks is a miracle man. He's never served a day behind bars."

"What's the point, Velie?" Ellery asked. "I passed up my lox and bagel for this."

"The point is," Sergeant Velie said, "we been digging into Marcia Kemp like we had advance information, which we didn't, and by God we struck oil. You know what, Maestro?"

"Stop milking it, Velie," the Inspector said; he looked tired.

"No," Ellery said, "what?"

"The Kemp babe and Foxy Faulks—they're married."

"I see," Ellery said, and he sat down in the cracked black leather armchair he had forbidden his father to throw out. "Since when?"

"I'm way ahead of you," his father said. "I'd like nothing better than to be able to hold her on a charge of bigamy, but the fact is she didn't marry Faulks till after the divorce from Benedict."

"How accurate is your information, Velie?"

"We got a copy of the marriage license."

"Well." Ellery pulled his nose, by which the Inspector knew he was cerebrating furiously. "That does put a new light on Miss Kemp. And raises all sorts of interesting questions about Mr. Faulks. When can the happy couple be interrogated?"

"I wanted them here today," the Inspector said, "but Foxy is out of town. He'll be back late tonight, you sure, Velie?"

"That's what my source says," the sergeant said, adding less grandly, "My prize pidge."

"Well, I want Mr. and Mrs. Foxy Faulks here in my office at nine on the nose tomorrow morning."

At nine-five Monday morning Ellery strolled into his father's office to find the Inspector, Sergeant Velie (looking vindicated), Marsh (in his capacity of executor for the Benedict estate), an edgy Marcia Kemp (in a purple minidress and mod hat that emphasized her Amazonian proportions), and a man Ellery naturally took to be Bernie the Fox Faulks. Faulks was younger than Ellery had expected him to be, or he had the knack of looking younger; his was the sort of baby face that maintains its bloom into the fifties, then sags into old age overnight. He was undeniably handsome; Ellery thought it quite reasonable that a girl of Marcia's background and outlook should have fallen for him. The pretty hood reminded him of a young Rock Hudson—tall, lean, and on the boyish-faced side. He was just the least bit overdressed.

"You know everybody here but Faulks," Inspector Queen said. "Foxy, this is my son Ellery. In case you're interested."

"Oh, yes, it's a great pleasure, I'm sure, Mr. Queen." Foxy clearly decided not to offer his hand for fear of a rebuff. He had a dark, intimate voice suitable for a sex movie. For the next few minutes he kept sneaking glances at the civilian Queen.

"We were just discussing Miss Kemp's marriage to Mr. Faulks," the Inspector said, settling back in his aged swivel chair. "You notice, Ellery, I use her maiden name. She prefers it that way. Don't you, Mrs. Faulks —I mean, Miss Kemp?"

"It's usual in show business," the redhead said. The flush on her face seemed too deep for street makeup. "But I still don't get . . . Bern, why don't you say something?"

"Yeah, sweetie." Her husband shifted his feet; he had refused a chair, as if to be better prepared for flight. "Yeah, Inspector. We don't understand—"

"Why I asked you two down here?" The Inspector showed his dentures like the Big Bad Wolf. "For one thing, Mrs. Faulks, how come you didn't tell Chief Newby when he was questioning you up in Wrightsville that you were married again? You'd have saved us the trouble of digging the information out for ourselves."

"I didn't think it had anything to do with . . . well, Johnny and all," the big showgirl burbled.

"No? Mr. Marsh," the Inspector said, turning his smile on the attorney, "has Mrs. Faulks—as Marcia Kemp— been receiving a thousand dollars a week from Mr. Benedict since their divorce, and if so has she been cashing or depositing the checks, according to your records?"

"She certainly has." Marsh raised his attaché case. "I have every canceled voucher that went through Miss Kemp's bank right here—each made out to 'Marcia Kemp' and endorsed 'Marcia Kemp' in her verifiable handwriting."

"These canceled vouchers cover the whole period since the date of her undisclosed marriage to Faulks?"

"Yes. Up to and including the week of Johnny's death."

"Did she ever notify Benedict, or you as Benedict's lawyer, that she was remarrying or had remarried and that therefore under the terms of her agreement with Benedict the thousand-dollar weekly checks should stop, since she was no longer legally entitled to them?"

"She did not."

"How about that, Mrs. Faulks? That constitutes fraudulent acceptance in my book. I think the District Attorney's office is going to see it the same way, if Mr. Marsh decides to press charges on behalf of the Benedict estate."

"If I may put in a word?" Faulks said elegantly, and as if he were a mere bystander. Marcia sent him a long, green, dangerous look. "I never saw that agreement, so of course I had no way of knowing that Marcia's accepting the grand per week was illegal—"

Marcia made the very lightest choking noise.

"—but you got to understand, Inspector, my wife doesn't know about such things, she can't hope to cope —hope to cope! I'm a poet and don't know it!—with a bigshot mouthpiece, I mean lawyer, like Mr. Marsh; she's got no head for the smart stuff at all, she'd probably forgotten all about that clause, like you do when Mr. Right comes along—hey, baby?" He fondled her neck, smiling down. She nodded, and his hand found itself fondling the atmosphere.

"You've got an understanding husband, Mrs. Faulks," the Inspector said approvingly. "But I think it would be easier on you if you talked for yourself. You'll notice there's no stenographer present, none of this is being taped, and you haven't been charged formally with any crime. Our main interest is the Benedict murder; and while I'm not making promises, if it turns out this remarriage of yours had nothing to do with the homicide you'll probably be able to work something out about that money. What's your feeling, Mr. Marsh?"

"Of course I can't promise anything, either. I certainly can't commit the estate to overlooking Mrs. Faulks's having collected money from my late client under circumstances that look dangerously like fraud. But it's true, Inspector, that my chief concern is the murder, too. Cooperation on Mrs. Faulks's part will naturally influence my attitude."

"Look, bud, who's bulling who?" Marcia demanded bitterly. "What are you going to do, Al, take it out of me in blood a pint at a time? I'm dead busted and I haven't got a job. My husband's broke, too. So I couldn't pay that money back if I wanted to. Sure, you can haul me up on criminal charges, Inspector, and the way things have been going for me you know what? I wouldn't give a hairy hoot in hell if you did. It's also a rap your D.A. might find it tough to make stick in court. Bern here knows some real sharpie lawyers."

"Speaking of Bern here," Ellery said from the wall he was supporting at the rear of the office, "where did you happen to be, Bern, on the night of Saturday–Sunday, March twenty-eight–twenty-nine?"

"It's a funny thing you should ask that," Marcia's husband said in his sexy voice. "It so happens I can answer that quick like a bunny, which ain't—isn't such an easy shmear, as I don't have to tell you gentlemen. On the night of Saturday–Sunday, March twenty-eight–twenty-nine, it so happens I was one of six fellas picked up in a raid on a little private game we were engaging in in a hotel room off Times Square. I don't know what those meathead cops were thinking of, making a big deal out of a friendly poker session, just passing the time, you understand, like the boys do on Saturday night, have a few beers, a couple pastrami sandwiches—"

"I'm not interested in the menu," Inspector Queen snarled; he was glaring at Sergeant Velie, who was attempting the difficult feat of making himself look like a dwarf for having failed to check out the Fox's alibi beforehand. "What precinct did you wind up in?"

"I don't know the number. It's the one in the West Forties."

"You don't know the number. Faulks, you know the

numbers of the Manhattan precincts better than I do—
you've spent half your life in them! Velie, what are you
waiting for?" Sergeant Velie nodded hastily and jumped
out of the office. "Sergeant Velie's gone to do a little
checking. You don't mind waiting?"

Dad, dad, Ellery said in his head, as an ironist you're
still pounding a beat. It was a lost cause, he saw, and
saw that the Inspector saw it, too. Mr. Faulks was
breathing without strain, as confident of the outcome
of the sergeant's telephone call as a roulette dealer
presiding over a fixed wheel. True, there was a trace
of anxiety on his wife's face; Faulks even patted her
hand, which was larger than his; but this could be accounted for by a certain lack of communication between the recently marrieds. Once, when Marcia said
something to him in a low voice, he made a fist and
tapped her affectionately on the chin.

When the sergeant returned to whisper into the Inspector's ear, Ellery detected the twitch in his father's
mustache and saw his fears confirmed: the mustache
twitch was an unfailing sign of inspectorial disappoint-
ment.

"Okay, Foxy, you can take off with the missus." Their
speedy crossing to the Inspector's door was a thing of
antelope grace. "Oh, just one thing," the Inspector said
to the antelopes. "I don't want either of you even going
over to Brooklyn without checking with my office first."

"He was picked up that night as he claims?" Ellery
asked when the pair fled.

"Well, yes," Sergeant Velie said, trying to pass the
episode off as immaterial. "There'd been a lot of heat
from upstairs about Times Square gambling when that
Congressman who's always kicking up a storm sounded
off for the TV—seems one of his campaign contributors
got rooked in a crooked crap game and yelled for mama
—so the word came while you were on vacation, Inspector, to crack down, which the Gambling Squad

did. That's how come Foxy got caught in that hotel.
A stool gave the tip-off, but by the time the Squad got
there the lookout had flashed the signal and the boys
broke in to find Foxy and his lodge brothers playing a
hot game of penny ante. The lookout must have been
their bagman, too, because the detectives didn't find
any big bills on the players or the premises. Anyway,
the six were held for a couple hours at the station house
and let go. That included Foxy Faulks. He was at the
precinct between midnight about and two A.M. He
couldn't have got to Wrightsville by three-o-three without a spaceship."

"So there goes our break," Inspector Queen said
glumly. "Another blasted nothing. Just the same, Velie,
assign two men to keep their eyes on Faulks especially.
I don't like the smell of him—he's dangerous. Ellery,
where you going?"

"For a walk," Ellery said. "I'll get more action in the
street than I'm getting here."

"Who conned who into this, and whose friend got
popped?" his father groused. "Go take your walk, and
if you're mugged in some alley don't come crying to
me!"

"You sure about this, Barl?" Newby asked, tapping
the report with a skeptical forefinger.

"You know old Hunker," Officer Barlowe said. "I do
believe he's been sneaking out there, Chief. Keeping an
eye on the place. You hire Morris, you've bought yourself Old Faithful. If he says he seen lights in the house
late at night, I buy it."

"Anything missing?"

"Not that I could tell."

"Then why would anyone pussyfoot around in there
in the middle of the night?"

Officer Barlowe, who was new to the Wrightsville

force, decided that this was a rhetorical question and consequently kept his mouth shut.

"I'd better take a run out there myself," Newby decided. "Meantime, Barl, you keep an eye peeled on that place, and pass the word along."

The next day the chief wrote to Inspector Queen: "Morris Hunker reported seeing lights on in the Benedict main house Monday night, April 20, past midnight. The old man claims he investigated—he would!—but by the time he got into the house the lights had been turned off and he could not find anyone there. I then went over the premises personally and found no evidence that anything had been taken or even disturbed. Whoever it was was either being extra-careful or old Hunker imagined the whole thing; he is not as quick-minded as he used to be. I thought, though, I had better let you and Ellery know about this."

"She wants to see me," Al Marsh said over the telephone. "Naturally, I'm not going to see her alone. Can you be present, Inspector Queen?"

"Hold on a minute," the Inspector said. "Ellery, Audrey Weston has called Marsh for an appointment. Says she has something important to tell him concerning the Benedict estate. Do you want to sit in?"

"Tallulah Revisited?" Ellery exclaimed. "I certainly do."

"Ellery will come, too," the Inspector said into his phone. "You figuring on anyone else, Mr. Marsh?"

"Leslie Carpenter. If it concerns the estate it concerns her."

"When's this for?"

"Wednesday at two thirty, my office."

"Tomorrow?"

"Yes."

"We'll be there." The Inspector hung up. "I wonder what the blonde's got up her sleeve."

"I'm glad somebody has something up something," Ellery said. "It's being a most unsatisfactory case."

Marsh's office was off Park Row, in an old set of buildings that reeked of musty estates and quill pens.

On his original visit, Ellery had very nearly expected to see old gentlemen in Prince Alberts stalking along the corridors, and bewhiskered clerks in leather cuff protectors and green eyeshades toiling away on high stools in Marsh's office. Instead, he had found sharp-looking young mods in a stainless-steel interior, the latest indirect lighting, and a strictly functional office. Miss Smith, of course, was for all seasons.

"They're in Mr. Marsh's office waiting for you, Mr. Queen," she said, sniffing twice in the course of the sentence.

Mr. Queen's only reference to Manhattan's consti-pated traffic was by indirection. "How did they get here on time," he asked, "by B-52?", and allowed him-self to be ushered into Al Marsh's private office. Miss Smith immediately sat down in a corner of the room, crossed her formidable legs, and opened a notebook.

Ellery found one stranger in the assemblage, a man in his forties with eyes like steak knives and a complex-ion resembling barbecued beef, in the general getup of an habitué of the Playboy Club. This man glanced ac-cusingly at his wristwatch as Ellery entered, by which Ellery knew that he was present in the interests of Audrey Weston, at whose taut side he stood.

"I believe the only one you don't know is this gentle-man, Ellery," Marsh said. "Ellery Queen, Sanford Effing, representing Miss Weston."

Ellery was about to offer his hand when Audrey's attorney said, *staccato*, "Can we get down to it?"

Marsh waved Ellery to a chair and reseated himself, to light one of his menthol cigarets. "All right, Mr. Ef-fing. You do that."

Ellery began to pay the strictest attention after a

smile at little Leslie Carpenter and a nod to his father.

"From what Miss Weston's told me about John Benedict's will," the lawyer said, "there's a rather queer phrasing of a key clause. I'd like you to quote me the exact language, Mr. Marsh, of the clause that refers to this Laura."

Marsh opened the top drawer of his steel desk and withdrew a Xerox copy of the Benedict holograph will. He handed it to Effing.

"Your recollection was correct, Miss Weston," Effing said with satisfaction. "Benedict left his residuary estate quote 'to Laura and any children' unquote. Mr. Marsh, the phrase 'and any children'—what exactly do you take that to mean?"

"Any children by Laura," Marsh said.

"Ah, but it doesn't say that, does it?"

"What do you mean?" Marsh said, startled.

"I mean it doesn't say that, period. If Benedict had meant 'any children by Laura' it's our perfectly reasonable contention that he would have written 'any children by Laura.'"

"But that's nonsense," Marsh protested. "What other children could Johnny have been referring to but children presumably resulting from his contemplated marriage to this Laura?"

"To any children," and Effing bared his large and shiny teeth, "that Benedict may have fathered by any mother whatsoever."

"We know of no such children," Marsh said firmly, but beginning to look doubtful.

"You're going to find out about one of them, Mr. Marsh, in three seconds. Miss Weston, tell these people what you told me."

"I have a child," the blonde girl said, speaking for the first time. The stagey voice quivered a little. "Johnny's child." She had been sitting with hands clasped and head lowered, but at this statement she made fists

and looked up defiantly, her colorless eyes taking on
a gray sparkle, like jellyfish suddenly touched by the
sun. "And you don't have to look at me, Al, as if I were
a monster from outer space! It's the truth."

"Your unsupported statement to that effect means
less than nothing to me as a lawyer, as Effing will tell
you," Marsh said sharply. "For a claim as important as
this, the surrogate is going to demand indisputable
proof. And even if you can prove your allegation, in
view of the rest of that paragraph in the will I'm not
at all sure your interpretation would stand up in court.
As far as my considerable knowledge goes—speaking
not only as John Benedict's attorney but as his close
friend as well—he never so much as hinted to me that
he was the father of a child by you."

"He didn't know about it," Audrey said. "He died not
knowing. Besides, Davy was born after the divorce."

"Johnny didn't notice you were pregnant?"

"We separated before it showed."

"You never notified him you were carrying his
child?"

"Davy was conceived the last time Johnny and I
were intimate," Audrey said. "Right after that we separated and he divorced me. I had my pride, Al, and—
okay—I wanted revenge, too. I was goddam mad at
the way he treated me, tossing me out of his life like
I was—like I was a pair of old shoes! I wanted to be
able to tell him later in his life—when he wasn't a cocky
stud any more—tell him that all these years he'd had a
son he didn't know a thing about . . . *and wasn't going
to.*"

"Indeed, Mr. Congreve, Heav'n has no rage, and so
forth," Ellery muttered; but nobody heard him.

"Now, of course," Effing said smoothly, "with the
father dead, the situation is quite different. Why should
the son of the father be denied his birthright, and all
that jazz? I don't have to go through the routine, Marsh.

You know how surrogates feel about the rights of infants. Regular old mammy-tigers, they are. I'd say Miss Carpenter's got something to worry about."

Ellery glanced at Leslie, but aside from a certain pallor she seemed serene.

"Tell us more about this child," Inspector Queen said abruptly. "What's his full name? When and where was he born? Do you have custody of him? If not, where and with whom is he living? That's for openers."

"Hold it, Miss Weston," Effing said, making like a traffic cop. "I don't think I'm going to let my client answer those questions right now, Inspector. I'll merely state for the record that the boy is known as Davy Wilkinson, Wilkinson being my client's legal maiden name, Arlene Wilkinson—she took 'Audrey Weston' as her stage name—"

"Johnny didn't know that, either," Marsh said. "How come, Audrey?"

"He never asked me." Her hands were back in her lap and her blonde head was lowered again.

Marsh pursed his lips.

"Miss Weston felt she couldn't adequately bring up her child and at the same time pursue a theatrical career, too," Effing went on. "So she gave the baby out for adoption immediately—in fact, the arrangements were settled before the birth—but she knows where Davy is and she can produce him on reasonable notice when necessary. The people who adopted him are certainly as interested in securing his legal rights and insuring his future as the natural mother is."

"The fact that she can produce the child," Marsh said, "is a far cry from proving Benedict was its father."

"Then you're going to fight this?" Effing asked with an unpleasant smile.

"Fight? You have a peculiar idea of an attorney's responsibilities. I have an estate to protect. Anyway, in the long run it's the surrogate you're going to have to satisfy. So worry about impressing him, Effing, not me. I'll have my secretary send you a transcript of this meeting."

"Don't bother." Sanford Effing unbuttoned the three buttons of his sharp suit coat. A little black box hung there. "I've recorded the entire conversation."

When Audrey and her lawyer were gone, Marsh relaxed. "Don't worry about this, Leslie. I don't see how they can prove the boy is Johnny's especially now that she's admitted before witnesses that she never told Johnny about this Davy. That's why I was careful to pinpoint that part of her testimony. The will is perfectly clear about Johnny's intentions: if he was not married to Laura at the time of his death, his estate was to go to you, Leslie, period. Unless this Laura comes forward with proof of a marriage to Johnny, which seems very unlikely now, it's my opinion you're in the clear."

"That's one of the difficulties a mere layman runs into," Leslie said, "dealing with lawyers."

"What is?"

"Trying to get a meeting of minds that isn't all fouled up in quidnuncs and quiddities, or whatever your jabberwocky is. I'm not the least bit interested in the law of this, Al. If I'm convinced the Weston woman had a child by Johnny, as far as I'm concerned that's it. In my lawbook the boy would be entitled to his father's estate, not me. It's true I've been making plans for the money—a certain project in East Harlem I had my heart specially set on—but I'm not going to break down and boohoo about it. I've been churchmouse poor and largely disappointed all my life, so I can put all this down to a dream and go back to washing out my nylons and hanging them up to dry on the shower rail. Nice seeing you again, Inspector, Mr. Queen. And Miss Smith. Just let me know how it all comes out, Al."

And with a smile Leslie left.

"Now there is a gal," Inspector Queen said "—if I were, say, thirty years younger—"

"Almost too good to be true," Ellery fretted. When his father said, "What did you say, son?", he shook his head, said, "Nothing of importance," and began to fumble with his pipe and the tobacco discovery he had just made by mail in a Vermont country store. Everybody knew there was no particular harm in smoking a mild pipe tobacco if you didn't inhale. He got the briar fired up and drew a deep lungful of the aromatic smoke.

"That's all, Miss Smith, thank you," Marsh was saying; and Miss Smith stalked past the Queens to the office door. Ellery thought he detected a certain twitch of her hip as she passed him. "You know, there's an irony in this development. Benedict Senior's will, as I told you, contained an ambiguity that allowed Johnny to draw another five million every time he contracted a new marriage. Now Johnny's will—I wish people would take lawyers' advice about not trying to write their own wills!—also contains an ambiguity *he* didn't intend . . . I wonder about this Davy."

"We can be all-fired certain Audrey Weston has a kid farmed out somewhere," the Inspector said in the quaint slang of his youth. "She'd have to be an idiot to try to pull a stunt like this based on nothing but hot air. And Effing doesn't strike me as the kind of lawyer to take on a tough will case that could drag along in the courts for years without something good and solid behind it. If Effing's in on it, there's a child, all right. But that the child was Benedict's, that Audrey never told him about it . . . ." The old man shook his head. "I don't know how this claim ties in, Mr. Marsh, if it ties in at all, but one thing's for sure: we have to start with the fact. How do you plan to establish that the boy is or isn't Benedict's son?"

"I don't have to establish either," Marsh said. "Proving the child is Johnny's is Effing's problem."

"Effing," Ellery repeated with distaste. He unfolded from the chair. "*Un type*, definitely. What—or who—next? Coming, dad?"

In these days of universal holdups, muggings, assaults, rapes, homicides, and other public indecencies it is a seldom-noticed fact of urban life that there is one class of citizen for whom late-night strolls in little-frequented places of the city hold no terrors; to the contrary, he positively looks forward to his midnight meander in the park.

And who is this hero, this paragon of courage? Some holder of the black belt? A just-returned Congressional Medal of Honor winner, schooled to the wiliest tricks of Charlie? Alas, no. He is the robber, mugger, assailant, rapist, or man-slaughterer himself, who, like the vampire bat hanging in its cave, finds warmth and security where simpler creatures feel a shivering fear.

Which explains why, in an early hour of Friday, April 24—"estimated as on or about 2:00 A.M.," was the way a detective noted it later in his report—Bernie Faulks Walked into Central Park (East) by the Fifth Avenue entrance immediately south of the Museum of Art, and made his way with confidence to a certain clump of bushes behind the building, where he settled himself in the tallest one and at once merged with the shrubbery and the night.

If Marcia Kemp's husband felt any fears, they were certainly not of the dark or of nightmarish things like switchblades at his throat; that side of the street had been thoroughly explored territory to him since his boyhood.

Still, there was tension in the way he stood and waited.

The moon was well down in the overcast sky; there

was little light in the shadow of the museum; the air insinuated a sneaky chill.

Faulks wore no topcoat. He began to shiver.

And wait.

He shivered and waited for what seemed to him an hour. It was really ten minutes later that he saw something take shape on the lamplit walk he was watching. It held its form for a moment, then glided into the shadow of the museum and headed his way. Faulks stood quite still now.

"You there?" its voice whispered.

The tension left him at once. "You bring the bread?"

"Yes. Where are you? It's so dark—"

Faulks stepped unhesitatingly out of his bush. "Give it to me."

He extended his hand.

There are soundless shrieks in the darkness of such moments, a dread implosion of more than mortal swiftness, that inform and alarm. Faulks experienced these even as the newcomer did indeed give it to him— a bulbous envelope, and immediately something else. For the Fox made as if to turn and run.

But he was too late, the knife had already sunk into his belly, blade up.

Faulks groaned, his knees collapsed.

The knifer held the weapon steady as the dying man fell. The weight of his body helped it slice down on the blade.

With the other hand Faulks's assailant took back the envelope.

The knife landed almost carelessly on the body.

The murderer of Marcia's husband stripped off rubber gloves, thrust gloves and envelope deeply away, then fled in a stroll northward toward an exit different from the place of entry . . . to a hurrisome eye just another foolhardy New Yorker defying the statistics of Central Park's nighttime crime.

"Ellery? I'm over here."

Ellery went through the police line, blinking in the spotlights, to where his father was talking to a uniformed man. The man saluted and left to join the group of technicians, scooter men, and other officers around the body.

"That was the Park patrolman who found the body," the Inspector said. "You took your time getting here."

"I'm not exactly full of zap at four o'clock in the morning. Anything?"

"Not yet." And the Inspector went into a song and dance—a song of profanity and a dance of rage—and it was as if he had been saving it all up for his son's arrival, preferring the thickness of blood to the thin edge of bureaucratic protocol. "Somebody's going to catch it for this! I gave orders Bernie Faulks was to be staked out around the clock!"

"How did he get away from his tail, and when?"

"Who knows when if we don't know how? Probably over the roofs of next-door apartment buildings. Velie had men posted back and front. Roof—nobody. I'll have his hide!"

"Aren't you the one who's always beefing about the manpower shortage in your department?" Ellery said. "Velie's too old a hand to slip up on a routine thing like that unless he simply had no one to assign to the roof."

The Inspector confided in his mustache. So all right. That was the case. Helping that cow-pasture chief out. And at half-rations personnelwise. The truth was—he almost said it in audible accusation—it was all Ellery's fault. For dragging him up to Wrightsville in the first place.

"What?" the Inspector said.

"I said," Ellery repeated, "that this could be a coincidence."

"How's that again?"

"Faulks was one of the bad guys from puberty. Who

knows what enemies he's made? I'm betting you'll find them crawling back under every second rock. My point is, dad, his murder tonight could have nothing to do with the Benedict case."

"That's right."

"But you don't buy it."

"That's right," the Inspector said again. "Any more than you."

There was a flurry of sorts just beyond the lighted area. The bulk of Sergeant Velie emerged suddenly into the glare with his right hand decorously anchored on Marcia Kemp Faulks's left elbow. She made the sergeant look like a normal-sized man.

The Inspector hurried over, followed at a 4 A.M. pace by Ellery.

"Has Sergeant Velie told you what's happened, Mrs. Faulks?"

"Just that Bern is dead." She was inner-directed rather than shattered by grief, Ellery thought; or she was in shock. He did not think she was in shock. She had got into wide-bottomed slacks and a nautical shirt and thrown a short leather coat over her shoulders. She had not stopped to make up. There were traces of cream on her cheeks and a towel was wrapped turban-fashion about her head. She was trying not to look over toward the group of officers. "How did it happen, Inspector Queen?"

"He was knifed."

"Knifed." The redhead blinked. "Murdered? . . . Murdered."

"It could be hara-kiri," the Inspector said flatly. "If he was Japanese, that is. Yes, Mrs. Faulks, murdered, with a switchblade his killer had the nerve to drop on the body, it's so common and untraceable. And you can bet without fingerprints. Are you up to identifying your husband?"

"Yes." It was almost as if Marcia had said, Of course, what a silly question.

They walked over to the group—detectives from Homicide, Manhattan North, the Park precinct—the officers stepped back, and the widow looked down at her late spouse without hesitation or fear or anguish or revulsion or anything else visibly human, so far as Ellery and his father could determine. Perhaps it was because she was emotionally disciplined, or the victim was not gruesome. The doctor from the Medical Examiner's office, who was off to one side packing up, had covered everything but the head, and he had closed the eyes and mouth after the photographer took his pictures.

"That's Bern, that's my husband," Marcia said, and did not turn immediately away, which was odd, because they almost always did—one look and let me out —but not Marcia Kemp, apparently she was made of crushed rock; she looked down at him for a full thirty seconds more, almost with curiosity, then turned abruptly and finally away. "Do I go now, Inspector Queen?"

"Are you up to answering a couple of questions, Mrs. Faulks?" he asked, very kindly.

"Not really. I'm pooped, if you don't mind."

"Just a couple."

She shrugged.

"When did you see your husband last?"

"We had dinner around seven thirty, eight o'clock. At home. I wasn't feeling well, so I went right to bed—"

"Oh? Didn't have to call a doctor?"

"It isn't that kind of unwell, Inspector. I get clobbered once a month."

"So you didn't see him again?"

"That's right. I dropped off to sleep. I'd taken a pill."

"Did you happen to hear him leave your apartment?"

"No."

"So you have no idea what time he left?"

"No. Please, Inspector. That's more than a couple, and I've got cramps."

"Just a couple more, and you're through. Did Bern say anything to you last night about having to meet somebody, or having to go out, anything like that?"

"No."

"Was he in trouble of some kind?"

"I don't know. Bern was pretty uptight about his affairs."

"Even with you?"

"Especially with me. He says to me—he used to say to me—the less you know the less you'll worry."

Ellery said, "Who wanted to kill him, Marcia?"

She had forgotten he was there, or perhaps she had not known. It was he rather than his question that startled her. "Ellery. I don't know of anybody. I really don't."

"Could it be he welshed on a gambling debt?" the Inspector suggested. "Or got in bad some other way with one or another of his playmates?"

She shook her head. "I really don't."

"Do you have any idea why he was knifed? Any at all?"

"None at all."

"Okay, Mrs. Faulks. Velie, take her home—just a minute. Doc?" He took Dr. Prouty's brisk young staff doctor aside. Ellery strolled along. "What's the verdict?"

"I set the time of death on a prelim estimate as around two A.M., give or take a half hour."

"Any reason to suspect the knifing might not have been the cause of death?"

"Didn't you see that belly of his?" the young man from the M.E.'s office said. "Though of course we'll find out for sure on the p.m."

"Nothing else?"

"Not a thing. Anything here?"

"Not so far. If you ask me, Doc, we won't find so much as a bruised blade of grass. An operator cool enough to leave the sticker on the body for us isn't going to lose his monogrammed cigaret case on his way out."

"Okay, Inspector?" asked Sergeant Velie.

The Inspector nodded, and Velie marched the big widow away. The young doctor waved and trudged off.

Ellery said, "She lied in her capped teeth."

"Your manly intuition?" his father inquired.

"I'm the son of my old man. You didn't believe her, either."

"You said it, I didn't. She knows something, Ellery."

"We're communicating again after a gap in the generations. What led you to your conclusion, Inspector Queen?"

"Marcia's not the type gal to know so little about her hubby's affairs. She worked Vegas a long time. She knows these bums, and she'd make mighty sure she kept tabs on Foxy."

"Exactly my reasoning. The only puzzle about Marcia is why she married him in the first place." Ellery looked after the departed couple. "Could love possibly go so far?"

"I wouldn't know. Or if I ever did I've forgotten."

"I'd keep her on a short leash, dad."

"Velie will. We'll know everything she does and everybody she says hello to."

"How about Audrey? Alice? Marsh?"

"They'll be checked right off." The Inspector shivered. "I'm cold and tired, son. Getting old."

"He had two hours' sleep and he's cold and tired," Ellery proclaimed to Central Park. "How decrepit can you get? Come on, grandpa, I'll take you home and tuck you into bed."

"With a toddy," his father said, hopefully.

"With a toddy."

By Friday morning the autopsy report was in from the Medical Examiner's office, and by Friday evening the little standing army of suspects had been checked off. Audrey Weston had landed a part in an off-Broadway production the previous week—it was tentatively called *A, B, C, D, E, F orGy*—and she had been home alone Thursday night, she said, hard at work studying her five sides. No confirmation. Alice Tierney, it turned out, had been in New York, not Wrightsville. She had driven down on Thursday and registered at a midtown hotel; she was in Manhattan, she said, to see Al Marsh on a matter connected with Johnny-B, an estate matter. "It's a long drive and I was tuckered out," the report quoted Miss Tierney. "So I went to bed very early." She had attempted to reach Marsh by telephone before turning in, she stated, but had been unsuccessful. (There was a record of her call at the hotel, and it was also confirmed by Estéban.) Marsh had gone out Thursday evening for a big night on the town, he said (he was in bad shape, the report said); his date was a stunning showgirl whose career had been launched in the centerfold of *Playboy* and who had zoomed from there into millionaire dates; however, in the course of their rounds she had ditched him for a certain Italian movie director who had muscled in on Marsh at a notorious disco—the details were in the Friday morning newspapers, featuring the director with his ample bottom ensconced in a bass drum, throwing up from a right to the solar plexus—after which Marsh had proceeded to go solo pub-crawling. Subsequent details were vague in his memory. Estéban had poured him into bed about 3:30 A.M. An attempt to log his course through the bars of after-midnight Manhattan proved spotty and unsatisfactory.

"It's just like in one of your books," Inspector Queen grumbled. "You'd think *once* one of the suspects would have an alibi that could be proved and eliminate her. Or him, damn it. But no, Foxy Faulks was knifed between one thirty and two thirty, and not one of the three can prove where they were—"

"He was," Ellery corrected automatically.

"—so we're back where we started from. Maybe you were right, Ellery."

"I was? About what? I can't think of anything recently."

"About Faulks's murder having nothing to do with the Benedict case."

"Nonsense."

"You brought it up yourself!"

"One has to cover everything," Ellery said stiffly, and he went back to pulling his nose. He was actually engaged in his favorite exercise in futility these days, trying to solve the mystery of the clothing thefts from Audrey Weston, Marcia Kemp, and Alice Tierney. It all seemed like ancient history by now, and he was beginning to feel like an inadequately funded archeologist; but the dig went on, secretly, in his head, where no one else could trespass.

"You know," Ellery said to little Leslie Carpenter, "if I hadn't met you in a case I'd ask you for a date."

"What a horrid thing to say."

"Horrid?"

"You imply that I'm a suspect in Johnny's death."

"I was only stating a principle," Ellery said, bathing sybaritically in the blue warm pools of her extraordinary eyes. "It's bad policy to enter into a personal relationship with someone you've met in the course of a continuing investigation. Muddies the thinking. Makes waves where dead calm is called for. By the

way, do you consider yourself a suspect in Johnny's
death?"

"Certainly not! I was talking about you."

"Let's talk about you. You know, I never thought I
could go for a halfpint, speaking femalewise?"

"You are *not* a groove, Ellery Queen!"

They were in Al Marsh's outer office, waiting for
Audrey Weston. Marsh was trying to get rid of a client
who was overstaying his appointment. Inspector Queen
sat restively nearby, munching Indian nuts in lieu of
lunch.

Ellery was about to launch himself splash into the
pools when the client reluctantly departed. Marsh
beckoned Leslie and the Queens into his private office.

"What's this one all about, Mr. Marsh?" the Inspector
demanded. "Seems to me I spend more time in your
office than in mine."

"It's Audrey, as I told Ellery over the phone." Marsh
swung a tier of law books out and it became a bar.
"Proving that the law isn't always as dry as it sometimes
seems. Drink, anyone? Don't usually indulge during
office hours—Miss Smith doesn't approve—but I think
I'll make an exception this afternoon. I'm still not over
that hairy night last Thursday, and I have a feeling I'm
going to need it." He poured a long one. "I can recommend the Irish, Inspector."

"I'm working," the Inspector said bitterly.

"I'm not," Ellery said.

"Les?"

"No, thanks," Benedict's heir said with a shudder.

"I mean," Ellery went on, "there are no regulations
on my job. Sorry, dad. Irish and soda, Al. Did you know
that the Irish invented whiskey? The English didn't
find out about it till the twelfth century, when Henry
the Second's boys invaded the sod and came back with
a few stolen hogsheads. Thank you, sir. To Henry the

Second's boys." When he had drunk a healthful draught Ellery said, "What does Tallulah want?"

"If you mean Audrey, she didn't call this meeting, I did." Marsh lit a menthol cigaret. "I've dug out some information on this paternity claim of hers. While we're waiting—did you know that Alice Tierney's in town?"

"We know," the Inspector said, sourly this time. "Is it a fact that she's visiting New York to see you?"

"Let's see, this is Monday . . . I saw her Friday, Inspector," the lawyer said. "I didn't tell you people about it because I knew I'd be seeing you today."

"I hope you aren't going to pull one of those 'this is a lawyer-client confidence' things," Ellery said.

"Not at all. Miss Tierney has come up with what the Little Flower used to call a 'beaut.' She had the gall to claim—get this—that Johnny promised her the Wrightsville property, the buildings and the land, as a gift."

"Oh, dear," Leslie said. "She sounds desperate."

"No proof, I take it."

"You're so right, Ellery. She has no evidence of any kind to back up her story. It isn't plausible on the face of it—did she expect me to swallow it? Anyway, I told her as politely as I could to stop wasting my time and hers. Yes, Miss Smith?"

Miss Weston and Sanford Effing had arrived, the blonde nervous, Effing narrow-eyed and sniffy, searching for clues like a bloodhound. When they were seated and everyone had got over the strain of being polite, Marsh (who had restored his wall before their entrance to its lawbook look) said, "Take this all down, Miss Smith. Is your tape recorder on, Effing? Good. I've done some poking into your client's allegation that she had a child by John Levering Benedict the Third whom she placed for adoption."

"And found that her allegation is true," Audrey's lawyer said severely.

"And found that her allegation—as it legally affects the disposition of the Benedict estate—is false," Marsh said. "There was and is a child, a male child named Davy Wilkinson—I have his adoptive surname as well, but in the child's protection I am keeping it confidential —but Davy is not John Benedict's son."

"He is, he is!" Audrey cried.

"Miss Weston, may I handle this?" Effing asked in a pained way. "My client says that he is, Marsh, and she ought to know."

"She ought to, but in this case Miss Weston seems confused. I have the date of birth from the records of the hospital where Davy was born. That date is eleven months and three days *after* the date of the divorce. Manifestly we have a marital impossibility. I think, Mr. Effing, you'll have to agree that there's no point to pursuing this further. Unless Inspector Queen wishes to do so?"

"If you're implying that there's attempted fraud here, Counselor," Sanford Effing stated icily, "I not only resent the implication on Miss Weston's behalf, but on my own as an attorney. I wouldn't have taken this case if I didn't have every reason to believe my client's claim to be the substantive truth. I do think she's been unwise to insist—"

"Ah, we get down to the old bippy," Marsh said, smiling. "To insist what, Effing?"

"About the dates. Please clear up that date situation, Miss Weston, here and now. You have no choice."

Audrey went into an elaborate hand-twisting routine. "I didn't want anyone to know . . . I mean, it was like —like stripping myself naked in public . . . ."

"Come on, Miss Weston," Effing said sternly, "it's too late for modesty."

"I said we were intimate for the last time before the divorce because I was ashamed to admit that Johnny and I had sex on a number of occasions after the—after

the decree." The North Sea-water eyes began to look
stormy. "But that's the truth, Al, so help me Almighty
God. We did. It happened mostly at my apartment, but
once in his car . . . oh, it's too embarrassing! Anyway,
on one of those *intime* occasions little Davy was conceived. My poor, poor. . . ." And the seas heaved and
sloshed, drowning Ellery's hopes that the blonde
would insert before the noun "baby" the traditional
adjective "fatherless."

A general cloud of discomposure moved in to over-
hang the office. Even Miss Smith, whose mouth had
been imitating a fish while she stenographed the pro-
ceedings, shut it and kept it shut with considerable
compression.

Marsh permitted the nor'easter to blow itself out.

"Audrey. If your attorney won't tell you this I'll have
to, for old times' sake if for no other reason. Even if
you can show that you and Johnny engaged in sexual
intercourse after your divorce, that would not in itself
prove that he was the father of your child. You know
that; or, if you don't, Mr. Effing certainly does.

"It's my belief that you've made up the whole story,
post-marital coitus and all. I'm reasonably sure I'd have
known from Johnny if you and he were sleeping together after the divorce. From some things he confided
in me—which I won't divulge publicly unless you force
me to—your story is highly suspect. It simply doesn't
tally with his feelings about you—do I have to say it?—
especially sexually."

"You have no right to make a judgment before all
the facts are in!" her lawyer shouted.

"I have every right to my personal opinion, Effing.
At any time. However, I see no point in denying it:
that's going to be my professional opinion as well, unless you come up with legal proof of your client's claim
that Mr. Benedict was the father of her child."

Audrey howled, "You haven't heard the end of this,

you shyster!" She was all the way off-stage now, being Arlene Wilkinson.

Effing rushed her out.

"Bad," Ellery said. "Very bad."

"I thought it turned out very well myself," Marsh said. "Certainly for old Les here."

"I'm speaking of Audrey's performance."

"Oh, I can't help feeling sorry for the poor thing," Leslie said. "Call me a square, but she is a mother—"

"A mother," Marsh said dryly, "who's trying a con game."

"You don't know that, Al. Johnny might have—"

"Not a chance, dear heart. See here, do you want this estate or don't you? I thought you had all sorts of socially progressive plans for the money."

"I do!" And the pools blazed from their depths. "What I want to do first—"

"Excuse me, Miss Carpenter," Inspector Queen said, jumping up. "The New York City police department has all sorts of progressive plans for my services. Mr. Marsh, from now on how about you don't call me, I'll call you? Okay? Ellery, you coming?"

"You go on ahead, dad," Ellery said. "I have all sorts of socially progressive plans myself. May I see you home, Leslie? Or wherever you're bound?"

But Inspector Queen's anxiety to get the Benedict case off his back was not yet to be relieved. Nothing was going anywhere—his staff was bogged down in the Faulks investigation, weltering in leads to enemies of Marcia Kemp's late husband whose name (as predicted) proved to be legion—and the old sleuth had hopes that there it would exhaust itself, so that he could get back to earning his salary for legitimate services rendered the City of New York.

Besides, it was impossible to live with Ellery these days. He went about with a fixed, almost wild, look,

something like an acid head on a bad trip, frequently
making noises that conveyed little but confusion. When
his father asked him what was upsetting him, he would
shake his head and become mute. Once he delivered
himself of an intelligible reply; or at least a reply com-
posed of intelligible components: "It's the women's
clothes, and something else. Why can't I remember that
something else? How do you remember what you've
forgotten? Or did I forget it? You saw it, too, dad. Why
can't you remember?"

But the Inspector had stopped listening. "And why
don't you take that Carpenter girl out again?" the Inspector said. "She seems like good medicine for you."

"That's one hell of a reason to take a girl out," Ellery
said, glaring. "As if she were a prescription!"

There matters stood when the call came into Centre
Street from Chief of Police Newby. Inspector Queen
immediately dialed his home number.

"Ellery? We have to run up to Wrightsville."

"What for? What's happened?" Ellery asked, yawning. He had spent a rousing night with Leslie at a series
of seminars on the subject of "Economic Solutions to
the Problems of Urban Obsolescence."

"Newby just phoned from up there. He says he's
solved the mystery of those lights old Hunker saw in the
Benedict house."

"Yes? What's the answer? Mice in the wiring?"

The Inspector snorted. "He wouldn't say. Sounds
miffed by what's going on down here. Or rather what
isn't. He seems to feel that we're neglecting him. He
just said if we wanted to find out what he's turned up,
we know where he is."

"Doesn't sound like Anse," Ellery said; but perhaps
it did. What did he know about Anselm Newby, or
anyone else, for that matter? Life was but a dream,
and so forth.

They got off the plane at a late evening hour of Sunday, May 3, and no Wrightsville police car awaited them.

"Didn't you notify Newby's office what plane we'd be on?" Inspector Queen demanded.

"I thought you did."

"At least Newby didn't ignore us deliberately. Cab!"

The chief was off duty; the desk man buzzed him at home, and the Inspector thought—aloud—that he took his sweet time getting to headquarters. The chief's greeting was correct, but unmistakably on the cool side.

"I haven't made up my mind yet what to do about her," Newby said. "On the one hand, I can't see the advantage in charging her—"

"Do about who?" Inspector Queen asked. "Charge who?"

"Didn't I tell you?" Newby asked calmly. "It's Alice Tierney my man Barlowe caught in the Benedict house late last night. She's the one who's been making with the midnight lights. It's a cockamamie story she tells, just wild enough to make me wonder if it mightn't be true. Frankly, I don't know whether she's gone off her rocker, or what."

"What story, Anse?" Ellery asked. "You're being damned enigmatic."

"Didn't mean to be," the chief said, Yankee-style. "Maybe you better hear it from her direct. Joe, buzz Miss Tierney's place and if she's home ask her to come down to HQ right off, the Queens want to talk to her. If she's out, try and find out where we can reach her."

"Why don't we go to her?" Ellery suggested. "It might be better tactics."

"She'll come," Newby said grimly. "After that yarn of hers, she owes me."

Alice stalked in fifteen minutes later.

"When the Queens command, little old commoner Alice obeys," she said coldly. It seemed to Ellery that she had been drinking. "It's all right, Chief, you don't

have to stand up with the royalty and be polite. Not
after last night."

"Miss Tierney, you were caught trespassing on private property. What did you expect Officer Barlowe to
do, kiss your hand? I could have charged you with
breaking and entering. I still can!"

Of the two, Newby was the more obviously agitated.
(Ellery guessed why in a moment. Alice Tierney was
a nice Wrightsville girl from a nice Wrightsville family.
Nice Wrightsville girls from nice Wrightsville families
were not caught prowling about other people's empty
houses in the middle of the night. Like most small-town
police chiefs, Newby was a defender of the middleclass
faith.) Not that Alice was serene. Her normally un-
heated eyes had acquired a glow not far from ignition.
She radiated hostility.

"Sit down, Alice," Ellery said. "No reason why we
can't talk this over without fireworks. Why have you
been going through Johnny's house when you thought
you wouldn't be seen? What have you been looking
for?"

"Didn't Chief Newby tell you?"

"We just got here. Sit down, Alice. Please?"

She sniffed, then tossed her head and took the chair
he offered. "You know by this time, I suppose, that I
told Al Marsh about Johnny's solemn promise to me?
That he wanted me to have the Wrightsville property?"

"Marsh told us," the Inspector said.

"Did he tell you that he laughed in my face, practically?"

"Miss Tierney," the Inspector said. "Did you expect
the attorney in charge of an estate to take a claim like
that seriously, backed up by nothing but your unsupported word?"

"I won't argue with you, Inspector Queen. With anybody. I'm convinced there's proof!"

"What kind?"

"A note, some paper or other signed by Johnny leaving the property to me. We got along beautifully during our marriage—lots better, he told me, than he got along with Audrey and Marcia. I really don't understand why he divorced me! He'd keep telling me how much he appreciated the nursing care I gave him after his automobile accident, how—entirely aside from our original agreement—he was going to leave the Wrightsville real estate to me. I naturally expected he would do it in his will. But he didn't, so I'm convinced he must have done it in some other paper, something he tucked away in the main house somewhere. I knew nobody would believe me—I appealed to Al Marsh against my better judgment. That's why I said nothing about it at the will session, and why I've been looking for the paper by myself late at night."

For the first time her voice rose.

"*I want it.* My weekly income is stopped, I haven't inherited that lump sum from Johnny—I'm entitled to salvage *something!* He meant that property for me, it's mine, and I'm going to have it!"

In a blink it occurred to Ellery—in the way a film shifts from scene to scene—that Alice Tierney was not the starched and stable angel of mercy of his comfortable characterization. The people who held feelings in as a matter of training and even nature were the ones who had most, under stress, to let out; and Alice was not far from the bursting point.

"My men and I went all through that house," Chief Newby said wearily. "You're not going to find what we couldn't, Miss Tierney."

"How about the guest cottage?" Ellery suggested. "Any chance that Johnny left something there, Anse?"

Newby shook his head. "Barl—Barlowe—and I searched the cottage today. Nothing doing."

"And if Marsh had found anything like that in Benedict's papers," Inspector Queen remarked, "he'd have to have mentioned it."

"I suppose I ought to check with him . . . maybe you ought to do it, Inspector." Newby added, not without a gleam in his eye, "New York, y'know," as if Manhattan Island were Richard Queen's personal property.

The Inspector found Marsh at home entertaining, from the background sounds of revelry. Ellery gathered from his father's end of the conversation that Marsh was not exactly overjoyed at the interruption. The Inspector hung up scowling.

"He says no such paper exists anywhere in Benedict's effects or he'd have let us know right away. He's sore that I even questioned him about it. Awfully touchy all of a sudden."

"That doesn't sound like the Al Marsh I knew," Ellery said. "Could he have fallen in love?"

"Then some girl is lucky," Alice said bitterly. "Outside of his damned sense of professional ethics Al is a pretty wonderful guy. *He'd* never promise a girl something and then forget."

"Forget is the word, Miss Tierney," Newby said. "That's what I'm going to do. Why don't you do likewise and run along? I'm not charging you with anything, so you're in the clear." He rose. "Do you have your own car, or do you want one of my boys to run you home?"

"I'll manage, *thank* you."

When she was gone Inspector Queen remarked, "That was a big nothing."

"Well," the chief said, "I'm sorry I dragged you gentlemen up here."

"I didn't mean it that way! Look, Newby, we seem to have got off on the wrong four feet—"

"It just seemed to me you ought to talk to her yourselves, Inspector, that's all."

"You were perfectly right. If police work was a success a hundred percent of the time, what fun would it be?"

"Plenty!" Newby said; and he grinned and they shook hands all around.

It was too late to book a flight back to Boston and New York, so the Queens plodded across the Sunday-night-deserted Square (which was round) and checked into the Hollis for the night. They bought toothbrushes and toothpaste at the cigar counter, washed up, and went down to the main dining room. It was late, the restaurant held about six other people, the Chef's Special (which from experience Ellery maintained was the only dish on the menu that was ever edible) was all gone, and they had to settle for two almost snorting steaks, which the Inspector's dentures could not negotiate. They got back to their room scarcely on speaking terms.

They were just taking their shoes off in the silence when the phone rang. Ellery said, "Big deduction coming up: Newby. Who else knows where we are?" and answered it.

It was Newby.

"If you're undressed, dress. If you're still dressed, stay that way. I'll pick you up in front of the Hollis in two and a half minutes."

"What now, Anse?"

"Tierney Rides Again. Barlowe just spotted her sneaking into the Benedict grounds. He radiophoned in."

"You know what that kook is doing?" the young officer exclaimed when they pulled up at the Benedict house; he had been waiting for them in a rhododendron bush. "She's trying to break into the whozis—that little stone house where Benedict is buried. I'd have stopped her, Chief, but you said not to do anything till you got here—"

"The *mausoleum?*" Ellery said; and they all ran, led by Barlowe with his oversized flashlight.

It was like something out of *Wuthering Heights* in the cloudy night.

She had pried the heavy mausoleum door open with a crowbar, and she was inside, in the light of a kerosene lantern, among the withered flowers, struggling with the lid of the bronze casket. It took Barlowe and Ellery to wrench her away, and Newby had to jump in to help hold her.

"Alice, please, you mustn't do anything like this," Ellery panted. "Why don't you be a good girl and calm down? We can go outside and talk this over—"

"Let—go—of me!" she screeched. "I know my rights! He promised me! The note has *got* to be in the coffin. It's the only other place it could be . . . ."

Her face was rigid, a mask of flesh, the eyes hardly human.

Officer Barlowe stripped off his blue coat and they wrapped it about her as a makeshift restraining sheet, lashing the sleeves at her back.

The four men carried her from the mausoleum on the top of the hill, across the meadow in the dappled dark, to the radio car. The chief relayed a call for an ambulance from Wrightsville General through the headquarters switchboard; and they held her down and waited.

There was little conversation. Her screams were too demanding.

May dragged by, going nowhere.

The hunt for the elusive Laura limped, hesitated, and finally came to a halt. Whoever the mysterious woman named in Johnny Benedict's will was, she had either taken refuge in a mountaintop cave or decided she wanted no truck with a murder case.

"In which event," Ellery said, "Johnny never married her, as we've maintained all along. So she gets nothing out of revealing herself except publicity, which she evidently wants none of."

"Unless . . . ," and Inspector Queen stopped.

"Unless what, dad?"

"Nothing. What thoughts I get these days are pretty wild."

"You mean unless Laura killed Johnny for a motive we have no lead to yet?"

"I told you it was wild."

"Maybe not so wild. It would explain why she hasn't turned up . . . I wish I *knew*," Ellery groaned. "Then I could get some work done." His novel-in-being felt like the cliffhanger of the old movie-serial days; it was tied helplessly to the track while his deadline came hurtling down on it like Old 77.

A, B, C, D, E, F orGy opened in a converted pizzeria on Bleecker Street to a scathing review in the *Post*, a series of witticisms in the *News*, silence from the *Times*, and a rave notice in the *Village Voice*. All went into detail about the third-act nude scene (the *Voice*'s description was matter-of-factly explicit about Miss Audrey Weston's blonde charms, which apparently overshadowed those of the rest of the ladies of the cast out of sheer volume). The play began to do an SRO business. Miss Weston, interviewed by one of the East Village papers, said: "Until now I have as a matter of professional as well as personal integrity rejected any role that called on me to appear in the nude. But Ali-Bababa's production is a different kettle of fish, dahling. (*Sure*, the interviewer interjected, *it stinks.*) It positively shines in this dull theatrical season. (*That's what stinking fish do, all right*, the interviewer interpolated.) I'm proud to be a part of it, clothes or no clothes." (*Stay in your pad and have your chick do a strip-tease*, the interviewer advised. *It's cheaper.*)

Marsh heard nothing more from Miss Weston, nee

Arlene Wilkinson, or from her attorney, Sanford Effing,
about the alleged paternity of Johnny-B *in re* Davy
Wilkinson, infant, adoptive surname unrevealed. The
consensus of Marsh, the Queens, and an assistant from
the District Attorney's office was that said Attorney
Effing must have advised his client either, (1) that
she had no case that stood a chance in the hell of the
courts; or, (2) regardless of the juridical odds, that
she did not have the scratch to finance what could only
be a long-drawn-out litigation (meaning chiefly the attorney's fee). For Miss Weston's sole source of income
these days, it appeared, was her salary from *A, B, C,
D, E, F orGy.*

The case of Alice Tierney took an unexpected turn
for the better. From her action and appearance that
Sunday night at Benedict's mausoleum, Ellery would
have sworn that she had gone off the deep end beyond
rescue; he had seen psychotics in the "dilapidated"
cells of mental hospitals with the same liverish lips and
wild-animal glare. But she made a remarkable recovery
in the psychiatric ward of the Wrightsville General
Hospital. She was a patient there, behind bars, for
two weeks under the care of Dr. P. Langston Minikin,
chief of the hospital's psychiatric service, after which
he had her transferred to a nursing home in Connhaven, where she remained for another two weeks
and was then discharged in the custody of her parents
and elder sister Margaret, who was also a registered
nurse. Dr. Minikin diagnosed Alice as a schizophrenic
personality, but the episode itself, he said, was a hys-
teric seizure, probably isolated, and not likely to be
repeated except under very extreme pressure.

Dr. Minikin told Chief Newby, "She seems resigned
now to the fact that Benedict either forgot his promise
or changed his mind—at any rate, that he left no written authorization or other record for the transfer of the
property at his death. She's a bit withdrawn over what
she considers the raw deal he gave her, but in my opin-

ion she's already managed a good adjustment, and in amazingly fast time. I don't believe Alice will do any more prowling, Anse." He hedged his bet. "She may do other things, but not that." It was not conducive to Newby's peace of mind.

But the really astonishing development of the month was the announcement that Marcia Kemp Benedict Faulks was taking unto herself a fourth surname.

It was not so much the fact itself that was to be marveled at in this age of multiple marriages as the identity of the lucky man. Ellery hardly believed the evidence of his eyes as he read the daily reports of his father's detectives and their confirmation in the gossip and society columns.

A romance was burgeoning between the ex-Vegas redhead and Al Marsh.

"Not that it's any of my affair," Ellery said at a three-way dinner in a hideaway East Side restaurant one night toward the end of May, "but how in Cupid's name did it happen? I never caught even a glimpse between you and Marcia of any romantic interest. On the contrary, I thought you disliked each other."

Marcia's hand groped, and Marsh engulfed it.

"You learn to hide things," the lawyer smiled. "Especially when you're the attorney in the triangle, and more especially when what you have to cover up is the McCoy."

"Triangle?" Ellery said. "You and Marcia—behind Johnny's back?"

Marsh's smile widened.

"Hardly," Marcia said. "I found out that Al ought to be carrying an Equity card. I thought he detested me. That's why I always tried to give him a hard time. You know how broads are."

"Look," Marsh said. "I couldn't cut in on Johnny either for personal or professional reasons. I had to suppress my feelings. I shoved them so deep I was hardly aware I had them, or I'd have married Marcia soon after Johnny divorced her. He met her through me, you know. I was in love with her when to Johnny all she was was a marriage of convenience."

The redhead squeezed his hand. "I know it's only a few weeks since Bernie died, but that marriage was from hunger—I was on the rebound from Johnny, I'd known Bernie Faulks in the Vegas crowd, and you've got to admit Bern was loaded with S.A. . . . ."

"You don't have to apologize, dear heart," Marsh said. "It was a mistake, Ellery, and Marcia and I see no reason to waste any more of our lives. Dessert, baby?" he asked her as the waiter hovered.

"Gawd, no! A bride has to think of her architecture, especially when she's built like the George Washington Bridge to start with."

Further prying was obviously futile. Ellery gave up.

It was to be a private wedding in Marsh's Sutton Place duplex; even the date was kept from the press. The few friends Marsh invited—Marcia said she had none she could trust—were pledged to secrecy and asked to come quietly to the apartment at two o'clock on the afternoon of Sunday, June 7. At the last moment Marcia decided to ask Audrey Weston and Alice Tierney—"I know it's bitchy of me," Marcia said, "but I do want to see their faces when Al and I are hitched!" (To her chagrin Alice declined on the excuse of her recent illness; Audrey did not bother even to respond.) The only other wedding guests were Leslie Carpenter, Miss Smith, and the Queens.

The knot was tied by Mr. Justice Marascogni of the State Supreme Court, an old friend of the Marsh family. (Ellery felt an extraordinary relief on being introduced to the judge; he had been half expecting—when he heard that a judge was to perform the ceremony—the appearance of old Judge McCue, whose similar role in the nuptials that climaxed his last investigation had concluded on such a cataclysmic note.) But this time the marriage-maker came, performed, and left with no cataclysm at all.

Until, of course, about forty-five minutes later.

It was curious how it happened, the accumulating clichés of all such affairs—"Isn't it June today? She's a June bride!"—the June bride's hilarity when someone exclaimed over the first champagne toast after the man-and-wife pronouncement, "Why, now your name is Marcia Marsh. How quaint!"—and the acting out of the small roles: Judge Marascogni's unfortunate lisp, through which "Marcia" sounded uncomfortably like "Martha," as if the groom were marrying another woman entirely, and the sibilants in the marriage service seemed increased a hundredfold, making everyone nervous anticipating the next one; the peaceful, almost imperceptible, way in which Miss Smith got smashed on her boss's champagne and eventually salted her glass over the death of her hopes (was there ever a homely secretary to a man as Marlboro-handsome as Al Marsh who did not secretly cherish such hopes?)—collapsing in Ellery's arms weeping her lost love, having to be laid on the groom's bed (by the bride) making Ellery wonder just how smashed she really was; the merriment over the wedding cake (not a creation of the great Louis, who was not a baker but a chef; an ex-colleague of his, who *was* a baker, had created it at Louis's command), the traditional awkwardness of the first bride-and-groom two-handed slice, and the bride's quite expert subsequent solo performance with the cake knife . . . until, as it has been noted, some forty-five minutes later, when the cake was one-third gone and Ellery found himself, through no conscious design he could recall, alone with it. Alone with it, the others having eaten their fill and scattered throughout the duplex.

The slices had all been taken from the two lowest tiers of the cake, leaving the upper tiers intact.

Highest of all, on the eminence, like triumphant mountain-climbers, stood the stiff little plastic figures of the bride and groom in their sugar-frosted canopy.

The little couple stared up at him crookedly. In slicing the cake Marcia had accidentally touched them and the canopy had slipped; they stood a bit askew.

Something popped in Ellery's head.

Like a tiny smoke-bomb.

The smoke drifted about, brushing his thoughts, dissipating, vanishing—the same elusive thing he had failed to grasp in Benedict's Wrightsville bedroom and elsewhere, later, in annoying retrospect. The something he had seen but failed to notice. The something he had not been able to grasp.

But this time he grasped it.

3.
The
Third
Life

They dropped into Wrightsville with the setting sun. Inspector Queen telephoned Newby from the tiny airport lounge.

"Meet us at the Benedict house," the Inspector told him. "Don't bother with a police car—I mean for us. We'll take a cab."

Chief Newby was waiting for them at the door. He had it unlocked and waiting.

"What's up, Inspector?"

"Ask *him*. Maybe you'll have better luck than I've had. I couldn't get a word out of him, and I still can't."

The chief looked at Ellery reproachfully.

"I'm not being coy," Ellery grumbled. "I've had considerable to think through. Shall we go in?"

They went in. The house was musty-smelling, and Newby went about throwing windows open. "Anybody want a drink?" Ellery asked. When the older men refused he said, "Well, I do," and he took an Irish neat, and another, then set the bottle down and said, "Let's go upstairs."

He vaulted up to Benedict's bedroom, and waited impatiently in the doorway.

"The answer was here from the start," he said. "That Saturday night. March twenty-eighth, wasn't it? Almost two and a half months ago. I could have saved us a lot of wear and tear. And Faulks his miserable life . . . well, it's all slops under the bridge. Come in, gents, and be seated. Don't worry about disturbing the evidence. It isn't the kind you can disturb."

"What?" Newby said, vague as a fish.

"Don't try to make anything out of it," Inspector Queen advised him. "Not just yet, anyway. He always starts this way. You sit down and you listen. That's what I'm going to do, Newby. I've had to do it a hundred times." And the Inspector seated himself on the bedroom's only chair, leaving the edge of the dead man's bed to the chief, who perched himself on it gingerly with an uneasy eye on the door, as if to orient himself to the nearest exit.

"You weren't there, Anse," Ellery said. "I mean in Marsh's apartment today, when he and Marcia were married. After the ceremony I found myself with the wedding cake, just the three of us—"

"The three of you?"

"The little plastic bride and groom and me."

"Oh. Oh?"

"They were, as usual, under a canopy at the top of the cake. And the groom fell off. Do you see?"

"No."

"It left the bride alone up there."

"Well, sure. So what?"

"So that was wrong, wasn't it?"

"Wrong?" Chief Newby repeated. "What was?"

"I mean, you look at the bride standing up there by herself, and it's obvious there's a missing element."

"Oh. Well, naturally. The groom. Anybody would

know that. Is that what you flew up from New York to tell me?"

"That is correct," Ellery said. "To tell you that there was something missing.

"From the beginning I've felt that there was a crucial clue in this room, a vital element of the murder, only I couldn't get my finger on it. Of course, when you think you can't remember something you take it for granted that it's something you saw, something that was there but slipped your mind. That lone little bride today told me my mistake. The clue in Johnny's bedroom here wasn't something I'd seen and forgotten, it was something I had *not* seen—*something that should have been here but wasn't.* Something which my mind unconsciously groped for, failed to find, and whose omission it registered.

"Dad."

"Yes, son?"

Ellery was at the clothes closet. "The room is exactly as it was on the night of the murder except that Johnny's body, the contents of the nightstand, and the three women's stolen articles of clothing aren't here now. Correct?"

"No," the Inspector said. "The weapon."

"And the Three Monkeys, yes. Everything else in the bedroom is as it was. That would include this wardrobe closet of Johnny's and its contents, wouldn't it?"

"Yes?" His father was intent.

"So what's in the wardrobe closet now is what we inspected on the night of the murder. Very thoroughly, I might add. Garment by garment. Remember? Even Johnny's hats, shoes—everything."

"Yes?" the old man said again. In the same way. Newby was still imitating a fish.

"Let's do a repeat. Go through the closet and call out whatever you see. As you did that night. Listen hard, Anse. See if you catch it. It isn't easy."

Inspector Queen began with the accessory items, enumerating: neckties, four-in-hands, ascots, bow ties, scarves, in all basic colors and combinations—

"Including browns?" Ellery interrupted.

"Sure including browns. Didn't I say 'all'?"

"Go on."

"Ten hats and caps—"

"Is any of them brown?"

"This brown fedora."

"Shoes?"

"Cordovans, alligators, suèdes—"

"Never mind the leather. How about the colors?"

"Blacks, browns, grays, tans—"

"Browns and tans noted. Overcoats?"

"Navy blue double-breasted, black with a velvet collar, cashmere—"

"Which color cashmere?"

"Tan."

"Brown family. Topcoats?"

"Charcoal, tan, chocolate—"

"Brown family again. That's enough to make my point. Step out of the closet, dad, and go through the drawers of the bureau there, as we did on the night of the murder. Take the shirt drawers first. Do you find any shirts in shades of brown?"

"Sure—"

"How about the hose drawer? That one. Any brown socks?"

"Plenty."

"You left out his suits." Newby was fascinated—puzzled, but fascinated.

"We did, didn't we?" Ellery said. As usual at such times, there was something of the actor about him, enjoying his performance. "All right, dad, start with Johnny's conventional suits. Which colors are they?"

The Inspector said sharply, "They're all in shades of blue and gray. Period!"

"Yes," Ellery said. "No browns or tans. That's what

kept bugging me, Anse, even though I couldn't identify it: the basic fashion color brown that wasn't represented in Johnny's suits, in spite of the fact that practically everything else in his wardrobe included articles in brown and/or tan."

"Maybe he just didn't bring a brown suit up here."

"Unthinkable. Johnny regularly made the Ten Best-Dressed Men's list. He wouldn't have worn brown shoes, or a brown hat, or a brown topcoat, or certainly a brown or tan shirt, with anything but a suit in some shade of brown. If he had brown accessories here, they had to be intended for at least one brown or tan suit.

"But I didn't have to make a deduction about it," Ellery continued. "Johnny did have a brown suit on the premises. I saw it with my own eyes. *On* him. The night he was murdered. He was wearing it when I was skulking on the terrace doing my Peeping Tom act while he held forth to his ex-wives about his plans for a new will. He was wearing the brown suit when he left them for the night and went upstairs to go to bed. That means he took the brown suit off up here, in this room, when he undressed and got into his pajamas. But when he phoned us at the guest cottage and we dashed over here and found him dead—*no brown suit*. No brown suit in his closet, as we've noted; no brown suit thrown over a chair or deposited anywhere else in the bedroom as you would expect after he'd undressed to go to bed—dad, you actually remarked on the neatness of the room, how no clothes were strewn about. You even specified what Johnny had deposited in the laundry hamper of the clothing he'd been wearing: socks, you said, underwear, shirt."

Newby muttered. "Then what happened to his brown suit?"

"That, Anse, is the question. To answer it you obviously must ask yourself first: who do we know was in this room later that night besides Johnny?"

"Who? His killer."

"Answer: Johnny's killer took away Johnny's brown suit. Q.E.D."

Newby threw an irritated glance at the Inspector. But Richard Queen was peering into the past. Or perhaps it was the future.

"Q.E.D. my Aunt Martha's hind leg," Newby said crossly. "It doesn't Q.E.D. a damned thing to me. *Why?* Why would his killer take Benedict's suit away?"

"You've just hit pay dirt, Anse. Let's go back. What do we know the murderer did after he entered the bedroom? He did three things we're now sure of: He killed Johnny. He left Audrey's gown, Marcia's wig, and Alice's gloves on the floor. And he made his escape with the suit Johnny had taken off in undressing for bed.

"Let's concentrate on number three—your question, Anse: why did Murderer, in escaping after his crime, take Johnny's suit with him?

"Was it because the suit contained something he wanted? No, because if that were the case he had only to take it from the suit and leave the suit behind.

"Or was the theft of the man's suit meant to symbolize 'a man'? That is, to point suspicion to the only other male in the house that night, Al Marsh? All the others were women—Audrey, Marcia, Alice, Miss Smith."

"Then why would the killer also leave the three articles of women's clothing?" the Inspector objected. "Those seemed to point to women."

"Disposing of that theory—right, dad. And there's another objection to that: we didn't even realize a man's suit was missing. If that had been Murderer's intention, he would have managed to call the fact of the missing suit to our attention. But he didn't."

"Can either of you think of still another reason?"

After a barren interlude Newby said, "You'd think

there'd be a dozen possible reasons for a thing like that. But I can't think of one."

Inspector Queen confessed, "Neither can I, Ellery."

"That's because it's obvious."

"Obvious?"

"What was it," Ellery asked, "that the murderer took away?"

"Benedict's brown suit."

"A man's suit. What are men's suits used for?"

"What are they *used* for? What do you mean, son? To wear. But—"

"To wear," Ellery said. "As clothing. The common, everyday reason. But why should Murderer need clothing in leaving Johnny's room after the murder? Surely he came there wearing something. Had he been splashed with blood—was that the reason he had to have a change of clothes? But Johnny's head bled remarkably little—we noted that on the scene, dad. Or even if some blood had got on Murderer's original clothing, that would hardly have necessitated an entire change—pants as well as jacket—in the middle of the night, in a darkened house. No, it must have been something else about what Murderer was wearing when he came to Johnny's room that compelled him to discard it and dress in Johnny's suit as a substitute. Do you see it now?"

Chief Newby looked helpless.

Inspector Queen exploded, "Hell, no!"

"But it's so clear," Ellery cried. "What was Murderer wearing when he came into Johnny's room that he might have felt he could not wear in leaving after the crime? You still don't see it? Well, what clothing definitely not Johnny's did we find on the floor—dropped there?"

"Those women's things." The Inspector was gaping.

"That is right. If Murderer came to Johnny's bedroom wearing Audrey's evening gown, Marcia's wig, and Alice's gloves, and for some reason decided to leave them behind, then Murderer would have required other clothes to leave in."

Chief Newby exclaimed, "One of those three gals, wearing the gown, the wig, and the gloves, came to Benedict's room, stripped, left them as clues to spread the guilt, and put on the suit Benedict'd been wearing to get back to her own room in." His face darkened. "That makes no sense at all. She'd have come in a dress or a kimono or something and just carried the three clues in her hand."

The Inspector asked slowly, "Are you saying it wasn't one of his ex-wives, Ellery?"

"You've answered your own question, dad. Audrey, Marcia, Alice—none of them would have planned to go to Johnny's room to kill him under such circumstances as to leave herself without clothes for her getaway."

"But Ellery, they were the only women there!" Newby said.

"No, Chief, wait a minute," the Inspector said. "There was a fourth woman on the premises. Marsh's secretary, Miss Smith." But when he looked at Ellery he said, "Not her, son?"

Ellery was shaking his head. "You're forgetting, dad, that we've postulated Murderer's going to Johnny's room wearing the stolen women's clothing. That means Murderer was the one who stole them in the first place. But when were they stolen? Audrey reported to us that her gown was missing as early as noon that Saturday. Marcia told us that her wig was gone not an hour later. And when I talked to Alice and she couldn't find her gloves, it was only midafternoon. In fact, it was during that conversation that Alice told me the others were preparing to drive over to the airport to meet Miss Smith's plane, which was due in, Alice said, at five thirty.

"So Miss Smith couldn't have been the one who stole the gown, wig, and gloves. Therefore she wasn't the one who went to Johnny's room that night wearing them."

"But there was no other woman in the house," the Inspector protested.

"Exactly."

Pauses have shades, like colors. This pause was unrelieved black.

The Inspector fumbled for some light. "But Ellery, there was only one other person there."

"Exactly."

"Al Marsh . . . ."

"Exactly."

And there was the pause again, less dark, more like a lightning-struck sky.

"Do you mean to say," Inspector Queen yipped, "do you mean to say it was Marsh—*Al Marsh*—who went to Benedict's bedroom that night all rigged out in a woman's evening gown, wearing a woman's wig and a woman's gloves . . . ."

"It's where the argument led us."

"But that would mean," Newby fretted, "that would mean—"

"—that we're investigating a case," Ellery said in a somber voice, "the real nature of which we didn't suspect until now.

"Al Marsh went to Johnny's bedroom that night in full drag, and what happened there forced him to leave the feminine clothing behind. He put on Johnny's suit to get safely back to his own room. Johnny's brown suit . . . when we find it, we'll have him."

"Find it?" the Inspector mumbled. "Fat chance. He'll have got rid of it long ago."

"I don't think so," Ellery said. "No, there's a good chance he may not have. Shall we go see?"

There was no flight out at that hour, and Ellery would not wait. Newby said grimly, "Take my car. I wish I could go with you."

The Queens drove all night, alternating at the wheel. They had breakfast in an all-night cafeteria on 1st Avenue and were at the door of Marsh's duplex a few minutes past eight o'clock in the morning.

"Mr. Marsh he's asleep, Mr. Queen," the houseman said, blinking in the entrance hall. "No can wake him up—"

"Is Mrs. Marsh with him?"

"She no move in here yet."

"Then you go on about your business, Estéban," Ellery said. "I'll take the responsibility of waking Mr. Marsh."

They barged into Marsh's bedroom without knocking. It was a spacious place of massive woods, hand-hewn and masculine. An eight-foot reproduction in marble of Michelangelo's *David* graced the room.

The lawyer turned over in bed suddenly and opened his eyes.

"Easy, Marsh," Inspector Queen said.

Marsh remained that way, in a half twisted posture, arrested in mid-movement. He looked formidable. His torso was naked and full of muscles and, surprisingly, hairless, as if he used a depilatory.

"What do you want?"

He sat up then. But he made no move to get out of bed. He drew his legs up under the red silk sheet and folded his heavy forearms over them, as if to hold them in check.

"What do you want?" he asked again.

"Johnny's suit," Ellery said gently. "You know, Al. The brown one he was wearing the night he was schlogged."

"You must be insane."

"Is it what *I* am, Al? Or what *you* are?"

Marsh shut his eyes for the briefest moment, like a child. When he opened them Ellery saw that they were old, bitter, and retreating.

"I don't know what you're talking about," he said in a mechanical way. "I have nothing of Johnny's here. Go ahead and look. And be damned to you."

His wardrobe closet was a roomy walk-in, like Benedict's in Wrightsville. Among the many garments on the racks they found two suits that, to Ellery's recollection, were approximately the same shade of brown as the missing Benedict suit.

"What size do you wear, Marsh?" Inspector Queen asked. "Never mind. According to the labels these are forty-four longs, Ellery. Benedict couldn't have worn more than a thirty-eight regular—maybe even a thirty-six. So these are Marsh's." None of the other suits was the color of Benedict's. "Any other suits in the apartment, Marsh?"

"This is your party." Marsh's throat sounded dry. He licked his lips. "I don't have to tell you, incidentally, Inspector, that I've seen no sign of a search warrant."

"There's one on the way," the Inspector said. "Sorry we jumped the gun a bit, Marsh. Would you rather we held up till the warrant gets here?"

The lawyer shrugged his heavy shoulders.

"I won't make an issue of it. I've got nothing to hide."

The Inspector looked the least bit worried. He glanced at Ellery. But if Ellery felt misgivings he did not betray them. He was going through the suitcases that were piled up in a corner of the wardrobe room. The cases were empty.

Ellery straightened up suddenly and stepped out of the closet. "I'm still partly in shock," he said, and drew his father aside, out of earshot of Marsh. "Of course it wouldn't be out in the open. He's hidden it in his clothes-hiding place."

"His what?"

"Marsh leads a secret life, doesn't he? That follows from what we've found out about him. During the day he acts the part of a normal man. But nights—some nights—and weekends—some weekends—he lives his other life. That means he has to have a hiding place for the clothes he wears when he's on the prowl."

The Inspector sprang back into the closet. He found the nearly invisible seam in the panel and the concealed spring in less than three minutes. Half the rear wall of the closet slid open.

Marsh had got out of bed and joined them in the closet. His pajama pants were shocking pink. His eyes were wild.

"Don't do that," he said. "Please don't go in there. I beg of you."

"Sorry, Al."

They were all there—street dresses, smart women's suits, cocktail gowns, evening gowns, high-heeled shoes, nylon stockings, hip huggers, an assortment of panty hose, panty girdles, silk panties, brassieres, slips. And at least a dozen wigs, in various styles and colors. And a vanity table loaded with a full freight of makeup materials. And a pile of gaudy magazines featuring handsome and muscular young male nudes.

And, among the gowns, the lone intruder, a man's suit, a brown suit, the brown suit John Levering Benedict III had worn on the last night of his life.

Under the law I have to warn you, *Inspector Queen began.*

Never mind, I know my rights, but I want to explain, it's important, *Marsh said. Moved by an obscure emotion, Ellery had tossed him a robe from the closet; he was very Marlboro striding about the bedroom, and it deepened Ellery's somberness. His father had died in an accident when he was very little, he explained;*

his mother, who never remarried, had been his evil genius.

She ruined me. I was her only child and she had had her heart set on a daughter. So she rejected my sex—not consciously, I'm sure; she was a Victorian throwback. Believe it or not she kept me in dresses, long hair, and dolls almost until I reached school age. And she'd had me christened Aubrey. I hated the name. You can imagine what boys made of it. At school I fought and licked every boy who made fun of me. I was big and strong enough to do it. I kept at them till they called me Al. Al it's been ever since.

But the damage was done. With no male figure to counterbalance my mother's influence—ours was a completely female household—whatever causes these things took hold and dominated me. I found out the truth about myself in my freshman year at Harvard. I'd long since wondered why I felt no particular yen for girls, like my friends, and had to fake interest; now I came to the realization that what I was feeling for Johnny couldn't be palmed off as ordinary man-to-man friendship . . . I never let Johnny know. The concealment, the need to watch myself, to pretend, cost me dear. It had to find an outlet somewhere. Inevitably there was an episode in a bar, well away from the Yard . . . then another, and another. It became an addiction, like heroin. I fought it with all my strength, feeling such shame and guilt afterward that I threw myself into college sports, especially wrestling. Until I realized why I had gone into contact sports. And gave them up.

Marsh went to the wall beside his bed and pressed something. A section of the wall slid away to disclose a fully stocked bar. He seized a bottle of bourbon and filled a water glass. He downed half its contents without lowering his head.

It wasn't only Johnny who never suspected. You

didn't, Ellery—no one did. I was ludicrously careful.
I never cruised anyone connected with the college,
even the ones I knew would be approachable. All my
pickups were made far off campus, like the first one,
mostly in downtown Boston. My great fear was that
I'd be found out. I suffered more than I can describe
. . . from the agony of alienation . . . the effort to dis-
guise my real wants . . . the need, the craving, to be
in the life.

Oh, God, *Marsh said,* you can't imagine what it's
like, the nervous tension, the inner turmoil, the loneliness—particularly the loneliness when I was putting on
my act in the straight world. And the persistent over-
drinking—it's a wonder I didn't become an alcoholic,
but I suppose my fear of self-betrayal acted as a brake
. . . I never considered for a moment going to a psychiatrist . . . I know I should have adjusted, as other
people have; accepted what I was. But I couldn't, I
just couldn't. For every hour of peace—why do I call
it peace? it was merely a truce—I fought an eternity of
all-out war.

When my mother died and I came into the family
fortune, I was even worse off. I now had the independ-
ence and the means to widen the area of my secret
life, but the dangers of discovery were also multiplied,
therefore the fears and shames and guilts. Also, no matter how much I engaged in the life, I felt incomplete—
what someone has termed "unfulfilled and unfulfill-
able." It's like compulsive eating, or any other symptom
of something wrong . . . the disgust I felt cruising for a
trick, the demeaning deals with hustlers, the sordid
hanging around public washrooms in hotels, railroad
stations, airport terminals, bus depots, angling for a
pickup . . . a marine, a drunken sailor, offering money
for an hour in some cheap hotel . . . and the greatest
dread of all, that while I was cruising at a gay bar or
beach or in some park—wherever people in the life con-

gregated—someone I knew in the straight world would run into me and spread the word . . . most hideous thought of all, some reporter who'd recognize me . . . . Do you know what the first commandment in the gay life is? "Thou shalt not be found out." You've got to understand that. I mustn't be found out. I could bear almost anything but exposure . . . I said a reporter would be the worst. That's not true. The worst would be a detective from the Vice Squad, playing the role of pickup . . . .

Marsh's delivery, which had begun in halting fashion, began to pick up smoothness and speed, like a partially clogged drain that had cleared. The purge of confession reddened and convulsed his face; his fists flailed away almost joyously at the pain of cleansing himself.

Forgive me for going into such detail, *he said, and downed the rest of his drink.* I'll get right to what you want to hear. *He set the glass down on the bar quietly and turned to face them.*

From the moment Johnny and I flew to that art auction in London, I had the exciting feeling that he'd suddenly guessed my secret. It wasn't for any reason I could put my finger on. Now that I have some perspective on it, it was an illusion brought on by the intensity of my desire for him. I talked myself into believing that all these years, while I'd been hiding what I was from him, Johnny had been hiding from me that he was secretly in the life, too.

It sounds absurd to me now, when I say it; there was really no basis for it. But, so powerful was the need, that's what I convinced myself of. I convinced myself that Johnny was giving me suggestive looks . . . inviting me to make advances . . . cruising me to come to his bedroom that weekend in Wrightsville after everyone else was asleep so that we could make love.

From the start of the weekend I felt a kind of crisis in identity that turned physiological with great rapidity. It sapped my usual control. That Friday night, when Audrey, Marcia, and Alice came downstairs all dressed up, something happened to me. Audrey's stunning evening gown with the sequins, Marcia's silly "fun" wig, Alice's elbow-length gloves . . . all of a sudden I was madly attracted to them. I had to have them . . . put them on . . . parade around in them. If we'd been in the city I could have used one of my own drag outfits, but we were in that damned backwoods town . . . And there was my beloved Johnny—the unsatisfied passion of my life—practically in my arms . . . signaling to me, as I thought, giving me the come-on . . . .

I slept hardly a wink that night.

By Saturday morning I was beyond reason or caution. While the women were out of the house or downstairs somewhere, I stole the gown, the wig, the gloves from their bedrooms.

I hid the gown and the gloves under the mattress of my bed, and the wig in the bottom of my wastebasket under a camouflage of crumpled tissues.

Marsh seemed scarcely conscious of them now, and the Queens settled themselves with great caution for the next few crucial minutes.

By late Saturday night I had no defenses left. My will power was gone. All I could think of was Johnny and how much I wanted him. I don't know how I got through that endless evening, Johnny's dreary spiel to those three. It was especially bad after he went to bed. I thought the women would never go up to their rooms. Finally, the last one did.

You have to realize I'd had a great deal to drink. I'd tried to hold the drinking down, but it had got to me. Maybe it was because of the excitement building up.

Marsh began striding again. Hands clasped, at one time wringing, another knuckle-cracking. Head lowered; rushing toward his denouement like a lemming.

I waited till I thought everyone must be asleep. Then I got the gown and gloves out from under my mattress, and the wig from the wastebasket. I opened the secret pocket in my two-suiter bag—I'd had it specially made—and took out the supply of makeup I keep handy there—a liquid powder base, rouge, face and body powder, false eyelashes, lipstick, mascara. The works. And I . . . changed.

His voice faltered before the last word. After he uttered it he was silent for so long that the Queens disciplined their breathing. Finally, he shook himself like a dog.

It wasn't a bad fit—you know how big they are, with Johnny's yen for women twice his size. Though I had to pass up shoes. Their shoes wouldn't have gone on my feet, and of course I couldn't put on my men's shoes, I'd have looked ridiculous . . . .

Marsh paused again, and Ellery thought how bright Einstein had been to insist on relativity. Marsh said he would have looked ridiculous in men's shoes. True, but how did he think he looked in a woman's dress? For the first time, as a result of Marsh's comment, Ellery truly saw him as not the Marlboro man but the transvestite.

I opened my door and listened. *Marsh said it liturgically, as if he were in communion with some deep, ineffable force.* The house was so still it sang—you know how they are sometimes in the middle of the night. I can remember my throat, how there was a gong pounding at the base of it. It was almost pleasant. I could even see pretty well; there was a good nightlight burning in the upper hall.

Nobody I could see.

Nothing.

I felt wonderful.

So alive.

I walked up the hall to Johnny's bedroom. I half

expected the door to open for me as I came up and Johnny to be standing there waiting.

But it didn't, and he wasn't. I tried the knob and it turned and the door swung with a creak like a haunted house, and I went in and shut it and it creaked again, and Johnny's voice said, "Who's that? Who's there?" in a mumble, and I felt around on the wall for the switch and then the room lit up and there was my darling sitting up in bed all sleepy and blinky, not naked as I had imagined he'd be, but in his pajamas.

Marsh's rhapsodic monotone, which had had the devotional quality, fell so low it became a mutter. They had to strain to hear him.

I think at first he thought I was Audrey, or Marcia, because he rolled out of bed and snatched his robe and put it on.

But then his pupils must have adjusted, because he recognized me. You could see his eyes do it.

They scarcely heard him at all now. He was clenching air with his fists and, feeling nothing, opening his big hands in a curiously supplicating way.

Could you speak a little louder? *Inspector Queen asked softly. Marsh looked at him, frowning.*

I've seen his eyes many times since, *he said with more volume.* At night. Even daytimes. I could read them like a neon sign. Recognition. Comprehension. And then shock.

They stayed shocked just long enough for me to compound my mistake. That stupid mistake. I wasn't thinking at all at that moment. It was sheer feeling.

The flowering, you might say. The bursting point.

I stripped off the gloves and wig. I tore the gown off. Stood there naked. And I took a step toward him and held out my arms, and that was when I saw the shock in his eyes turn to revulsion, absolute revulsion.

He said to me, "You filthy, filthy pig. Get out of my house."

Marsh turned his back to them and made little throat-clearing noises. When he spoke again it was to unoccupied space, as if he had wished them away and they had obediently disappeared.

I found myself saying some things to him then . . . I remember . . . about my love . . . my years of fighting to hide it from him . . . .

I knew it was worse than useless—his eyes told me that—but I couldn't stop myself, it all came out, everything, and all the time I knew it was a fatal mistake . . . that he wasn't capable of understanding . . . any more than you . . although I hope . . . I hoped . . . .

He never raised his voice. It was brutal. He was cruel, viciously so. The things he called me . . . unforgivable things from an intelligent, civilized man . . . even if he couldn't share my feelings, he'd known me so long, we'd been such friends. If I'd been a leper and deliberately infected him out of malice he couldn't have shown more hate, as if I were his enemy . . . . All the time he was cutting me to bits, the shame, the guilt, the fear—the panic—grew. All my years of being careful—successfully—thrown away in one uncontrollable act. In one night.

He was threatening to expose me.

I don't know why Johnny reacted so violently to what he'd found out about me. I hadn't really done anything to him except reveal myself for what I was. He couldn't handle the revelation. Maybe he had a deep-seated hangup about inversion. A lot of men do . . . as if they're afraid the same thing is buried in *them,* and by attacking it in others . . . I don't know.

I had no time to analyze Johnny then. I was too busy panicking.

He was threatening to expose me; and that would be the end of me. At that moment that was all I could think of—that, and shutting his mouth. The cast-iron Three Monkeys thing was on his bureau and the next thing I knew I found myself smashing him over the head with it. It was like a reflex. No rational thought behind it. He mustn't tell. I must keep him from talking. That's all I knew.

Marsh turned around and they saw the surprise in his eyes at the sight of them, and then the distaste, almost the contempt, as if he had caught them eaves-dropping. But even that drained rapidly out of his eyes, leaving them empty.

It never occurred to me that Johnny wasn't dead. I simply took it for granted. He looked dead . . . sprawled there . . . his pale, almost green, face . . . the blood . . . .

I opened the door a crack and looked out and my heart jumped. There was a tall girl on the landing in a dressing gown, about to go downstairs. She turned her head a bit, and I saw it was Audrey Weston.

Paralyzed, I watched her go down.

She was down there only a couple of minutes. She came back up with a book and went to her room.

I looked down at myself. I was naked. I'd forgotten. I began to shake. Suppose she'd seen me?

I'd hardly had time to feel relieved when Marcia came out of her bedroom—I knew instantly it was Mar-cia, because I saw her red hair as she passed under the nightlight—and she headed for downstairs, too.

I suppose desperation calmed me down. I hadn't dreamed that people would be wandering about the house in the middle of the night.

All I could think of now was getting safely back to my room. Marcia was downstairs—she might come back at any moment, as Audrey had. I didn't dare go the way I was, without a stitch on—that would be a dead giveaway if I were seen . . . and the thought of getting back into drag, the way I had come, was even worse. Suppose one of the women saw me in women's clothes? In *their* clothes?

Yet I had to get out of Johnny's bedroom.

There was only one thing I could think of, and that was to put on something of Johnny's. The brown suit he'd been wearing was lying on the chair. I managed to squeeze into it. . . .

Ellery nodded. Both shoulder seams of Benedict's suit were split open, a fact the District Attorney was going to appreciate.

At the last moment it came to me—fingerprints. My brain was working independently; it wasn't mine. No panic now. I felt nothing. I used the handkerchief I found in Johnny's pocket—it's still there—and wiped off everything I'd touched . . . the Three Monkeys where I'd held it, the doorknob, whatever I'd come in contact with.

I ran back to my own room.

I locked the door, took off the suit and packed it at the bottom of my suitcase. And washed . . . .

Marsh shut his eyes again.

He said in an exhausted, final way, There was Johnny's blood on me.

That was the body of it.

There were appendages. Why had he hung onto Benedict's suit?

"Was it because it had belonged to Johnny?" Ellery asked.

"Yes."

Queen *fils* regarded Queen *père*. The Inspector could only shake his head.

"You realize, Al, there's blood inside the jacket? Undoubtedly Johnny's, which got on your bare hide when you struck him and then smeared the lining when you put the jacket on for your escape. Didn't it occur to you that, with the blood types matching—Johnny's and the stains'—and the suit found in your possession, it was the most damaging kind of evidence against you?"

"I didn't think it would be found. Nobody, not even Estéban, knew about the hidden closet. Anyway, I couldn't bring myself to part with the suit. It was Johnny's."

Ellery found himself turning away.

Inspector Queen wanted to know about the marriage. "It doesn't add up, Marsh. Not in view of what you've just told us about yourself."

But it did.

On the night of the murder Marcia, who was occupying the room next to Marsh's, heard his door open and peeped out. He was in the full flight of his obsession and he neither heard nor saw her. As Marsh passed under the nightlight in the hall, bound for Benedict's room, Marcia got a full view of his face and, in spite of the woman's outfit and makeup he was wearing, she recognized him.

"Marcia's the only one I know of who for a long time had had suspicions about me," the lawyer said. "She's very shrewd and perceptive about such things, with her show business background and the years she's knocked about places like Las Vegas. At any rate, what she saw in the hall that night, she told me later, confirmed what she'd always suspected. If she had testified what she'd seen when Chief Newby and you people were questioning us, she'd have blown the case sky high the night of the murder."

But Marcia had foreseen an advantage in silence, and events soon repaid her perspicacity. The death of Benedict cut off her weekly income, and his failure to specify the expected lump-sum settlement in his holograph will left her without a penny. She confided Marsh's secret to the petty hood she had married after her divorce from Benedict, and Foxy Faulks grabbed the opportunity.

"Sweet setup for blackmail," Inspector Queen said, nodding. "She'd spotted you in drag, she certainly

guessed that you were the one who had murdered
Benedict, and you're a rich man. No wonder you killed
Faulks. You did, didn't you?"

"What else could I do?" Marsh said, and he shrugged.
"I don't have to tell you people how blackmailers oper-
ate. They'd have bled me white, and I'd never have
been out of danger of exposure." He had arranged to
meet Faulks behind the Museum of Art in Central Park
late at night, presumably for a payoff, and instead had
given Marcia's husband a knife in the abdomen.

"I figured that would scare Marcia off my back,"
Marsh went on, "out of just plain self-preservation.
She'd have to realize that if I was willing to kill Faulks,
I wouldn't shrink from killing her as well. Therefore
she'd fade out of the picture.

"But Marcia came up with a very smart counter-ploy.
She proposed that we get married. She pleaded a per-
suasive case. Our marriage would give her the financial
security she wanted, and it would give me the smoke-
screen I needed to hide what I was. A lot of us, by the
way, marry for precisely that reason. And she didn't
have to remind me that a wife can't be made to testify
against her husband, if it ever came to that. Well, we
never got really started, thanks to you, Ellery. She's
still preparing to move in here."

Ellery said nothing.

To which Marsh said a curious thing. "I wonder
what you're thinking."

"Not what you think I'm thinking, Al," Ellery said.

"Then you're an exception. If only people stopped
regarding us as some sort of monsters . . . let us live
our lives out as we're constituted, in decent privacy
and without prejudice, I don't believe this would have
happened. It would have been possible for me to propose, and Johnny to reject, without disgust and vitriol
on his part or panic on mine. He wouldn't have casti-
gated or threatened me. I wouldn't have lost my head.

We might even have remained friends. Certainly he'd still be alive.

"Poor Johnny," Marsh said, and was silent.

The Queens were quiet, too. A great change had come over Marsh in the past few minutes. He looked juiceless, squeezed dry of his vital constituents; he looked old.

Finally Inspector Queen cleared his throat.

"You'd better get dressed, Marsh. You'll have to come downtown with us."

The lawyer nodded, almost agreeably.

"I'll wash up."

He went into the bathroom.

They had to break through the door.

Marsh was lying on the tiled floor.

He had swallowed cyanide.

In the middle of the night after Marsh's suicide Ellery popped up out of sleep like a smoking piece of
toast, groped for the nightlight, kicked the sheet, and
ran to his father's bedroom.

"Dad!"

The Inspector stopped snoring to open one eye.
"Unnh?"

"Vincentine Astor!"

"Wha'?"

"Vincentine Astor!"

"Unnh."

"Nobody would have a name like that legitimately.
It's got to be a take-on, a phony—somebody's idea of
class. I'm betting she's Laura! Laura Man-something!"

"Go back to sleep, son." The old man took his own
advice.

But Laura Man-something the vanished hatcheck
girl of Manhattan's Boy-Girl Club turned out to be.
They found Miss Manzoni in her native Chillicothe,
Ohio, in the shadow of Mt. Logan among the mysterious mounds, putting books back in the stacks of the
Carnegie Library. She was living with her father, step-
mother, and a mixed brood of original and acquired
Manzonis in a pleasant frame house on a street of dying elms. Her father, Burton Stevenson Manzoni, had
been employed in one of Chillicothe's paper mills for
twenty-seven years.

Laura Manzoni was a surprise. She was not the bold,
platinum-and-enamel gum-chewer they had expected.
Pretty and stacked she was; but otherwise Laura was
softly chestnut-haired, soft-eyed, soft-spoken, and a
gentleman's lady. She had majored in drama at Ober-

lin, and she had gone off to New York for the predictable reason, with the predictable result.

For eating and sleeping money, when her grubstake
ran out, she had dyed her hair, bought a mini-miniskirt
and peekaboo stockings, applied a thick coat of theatrical makeup to her fresh Midwestern face, and
bluffed her way into the hatcheck job at the nightclub.
There she had met Johnny Benedict.

He claimed, Laura said, to have seen through her
masquerade "to the essential me" immediately. She re-
sisted his invitations for three weeks. Then they began
to meet after hours, discreetly; this was as much, she
said, at Benedict's insistence as at hers.

"Finally he told me he was serious about me," Laura
said, "and then that he loved me. Of course I didn't believe him; I knew his reputation. But Johnny was such a
charmer. He really was. He knew how to make a
woman feel she was the center of everything. And the
most he ever tried to do was kiss me. Still, something
about him held me back. . . .

"I suppose I wanted very much to be convinced, but
I kept putting him off. It's hard for a girl like me to
believe what a man like Johnny tells her—a young and
handsome multimillionaire—even, or maybe especially,
if he doesn't make passes or propositions. What made
it harder . . . he kept talking about our getting married. As if it were all settled. Johnny couldn't believe
any girl he was rushing would turn him down. I kept
telling him I wasn't sure, I needed time, and he kept
saying that time was for clock punchers, that we were
going to be married right away, that he'd made all
his plans, and that sort of thing."

"Did Mr. Benedict ask you to sign any sort of agreement?" asked the plainclothesman whom Chief Newby
had sent to Chillicothe to question her.

"Agreement?" Laura shook her head. "I wouldn't even
if he had, regardless of what it was. As I say, I just

wasn't sure of myself. Or, for that matter, of Johnny. In fact, when he told me he had to go up to Wrightsville—"

"Then you knew about Mr. Benedict's get-together with his ex-wives the weekend of March twenty-eighth?"

"He didn't say why he was going specifically, or who'd be there. Just that he had some unfinished business, as he called it, to clean up. That was the trouble."

"Trouble, Miss Manzoni? What trouble?"

It then came out. Laura's uncertainty about Benedict's sincerity and motives trapped her into an act that had preyed on her conscience ever since. His vagueness about the purpose of his Wrightsville weekend had fed her misgivings; with Laura's middleclass, Midwestern upbringing—in spite of what she had always considered her emancipation from it—all she could think of was a "love nest" and "another woman." Hating her suspicions, but telling herself that it was a test that would decide the issue of Johnny Benedict for her one way or the other, she had rented a car that Saturday and driven up to Wrightsville.

"I don't believe I'd even thought through what I was going to do when I got there," the girl said. "Maybe some grandiose visions of finding him there with a chick, telling him off in a curtain speech, and making a glorious exit. When I did get there—I was actually turning into Johnny's driveway—I was suddenly overwhelmed with shame. I saw how wrong the whole thing was in a kind of reverse rush of feeling, the way you do sometimes. I hadn't trusted Johnny, I didn't trust him then, and I knew I never would or could. So I turned the car around and drove right back to New York. And that Sunday morning—I was too upset to go to bed—I heard over the radio that Johnny'd been murdered during the night."

Fear—that she might have been seen outside the

house or in Wrightsville or the vicinity and at once involved in the murder—sent Laura fleeing to Chillicothe and home. She had never told her family about her link to the young society man whose name and photograph were in the newspapers and newscasts. When the story broke about the mysterious Laura named as Benedict's beneficiary in his holograph will in the event of their marriage, she had needed no attorney to tell her that she had no claim on the Benedict estate, since the event had never taken place.

She would have fought identification as the missing Laura, Laura said, with tooth and nail if Benedict's murder had not been solved.

"I've had a boy friend here in Chillicothe—on the next block, in fact—since childhood," Laura Manzoni said to Newby's emissary, "who's wanted to marry me since we graduated from high school. We're on the verge of setting the date. But his folks are real hardshell Baptists and, while Buell would stick by me if I were dragged through the papers and TV, they'd make things very unpleasant for us. Can you keep my name out of this? *Please?*"

They kept her name out of it . . . "the last woman in Benedict's life," Inspector Queen repeated. "Isn't that what he called her that Saturday night?"

"He was wrong," Ellery said dourly. "Laura Manzoni wasn't the last woman in Johnny's life."

"She wasn't?"

"She wasn't."

"But then who was?"

Ellery held his drink up to the light and squinted at it. It was straight sour-mash bourbon. He made a face and tossed it down like medicine.

"Al Marsh."

"Marsh," Inspector Queen said, dropping the news magazine. He had been reading about Marsh's funeral, and the recapitulation of the events that had led up to it. In the new freedom of expression enjoyed by the press, the story was explicit, too much so to the Inspector's old-fashioned taste. "I still can't get a feeling of reality about it."

"Why not?" Ellery demanded. "In your time you've investigated whole botanical gardens of men like Marsh, dad. Every police officer has. You know that."

"But it's the first time I was involved in a case with one on a personal basis. Marsh looked and acted like such a *man* of a man, if you know what I mean. Maybe if he'd been the obvious kind—"

"In his own way he was."

The old man stared.

"His apartment," Ellery said. "He practically threw his secret in your face."

"If so, I didn't get it."

"There's an excuse for you. You weren't entertained there."

"You mean all that manly type furniture, and the athletic equipment and so forth? Coverups?"

Ellery smiled faintly. "They were coverups in Marsh's case, certainly, but hardly clues, or society would really have a problem! No, it was a clue like a sequoia—so tall and broad I missed it entirely. His music library—more Tchaikovsky and Beethoven than anyone else. His rare and first editions—Proust, Melville, Chris Marlowe, Gide, Verlaine, Henry James, Wilde, Rimbaud, Walt Whitman. His art books—chiefly da Vinci and Michelangelo. The busts he had on display—Alexander the Great, Plato, Socrates, Lawrence of Arabia, Virgil, Julius Caesar, Catullus, Horace, Frederick the Great, von Humboldt, Lord Kitchener."

"So what?" his father said, bewildered.

"You Victorian innocent! All those historic gentlemen had, or are reputed to have had, one thing in common . . . along with Aubrey alias Al Marsh."

The Inspector was silent. Then he said feebly, "Julius Caesar? I didn't know it about *him*."

"We don't know it about most. An Englishman named Bryan Magee wrote a book a few years ago that he called *One in Twenty*. In it he makes the statement that the idea that deviates can necessarily be recognized as such is a myth. The overwhelming majority of them, of both sexes, Magee says—and he did a vast job of research in preparation for two TV documentaries he presented on the subject—are outwardly indistinguishable from normally sexed people. It can be anybody—the brawny fellow working beside you in the office, your bartender, the guy next door, the friend you play bridge with every Thursday night, the cop on your beat, or your mousy Cousin Horace. One in twenty, dad—that's the current statistic. And that figure may be far too conservative. Kinsey claimed it was one in ten. . . . Anyway, there it was, the clue in Marsh's living room. Staring me in the mandibles. Like the figleafless *David* he enshrined in his bedroom, eight feet tall and naked as the day Michelangelo lovingly made the original . . . I can't say I'm proud of my role in this caper, dad. And not only for that reason."

"You mean there was another clue, too?"

"Clue is hardly the word. It was—excuse the pun—almost a dead giveaway. Johnny *told* me who'd done it."

"Told you?" Inspector Queen scratched his mustache angrily. "Told you, Ellery? How? When?"

"As he was dying. When he came to from the beating, after Marsh left him for dead, Johnny realized he had only a short time to live. In those last few moments preceding death he experienced one of those infinities of clarity, when time stretches beyond its ordinary limits and the dying brain performs prodigies of thought in what we three-dimensional air-breathers call seconds.

"He knew there were no writing materials handy—you'll recall you and I searched when we got there and failed to find any. Yet he wanted desperately to let us know who had attacked him, and why. So he managed somehow to use the extension phone to the cottage."

Ellery frowned into the past. "Johnny knew my first question—anyone's first question under the circumstances—would be: who did it? But in that timeless flash of brilliance, as he was groping for the phone, he found himself in a fantastic situation."

"Fantastic situation?" The Inspector frowned into the present. "What do you mean?"

"What I mean is," Ellery said, "how could he tell me who had murdered him?"

"How could he tell you? What are you talking about, Ellery? All he had to do was say the killer's name."

"All right," Ellery said. "Say it."

"Al."

"Oh, but that could have been an uncompleted attempt to say 'Alice.' How would we have known it wasn't?"

"Oh," the Inspector said. "Well, then Marsh."

"Could have been the unfinished start of 'Marcia.'"

The old man began to look interested. "I see what you mean! . . . Then Marsh's christening name, Aubrey. You'd have understood that."

"Would I, dad? In light of Johnny's speech impediment? How could I ever have been sure he hadn't meant to say 'Audrey'?"

"Huh." The Inspector thought deeply. "Huh!" he said. "Funny problem, at that. . . . How about the word 'lawyer'? No possible mixup there. Marsh was the only lawyer Benedict could have meant."

"Johnny was probably thinking in terms of names only. But assuming he thought of 'lawyer,' see what a bind he found himself in. He was intending to marry Laura, a girl he loved; her name was in the will he'd given you to put in your pocket. If he said 'lawyer,' we might have mistaken the word for the name—'lawyer' for 'Laura'! Remember, he had great difficulty pronouncing the letter *r*. Between the impediment and his dying diction, it was too great a risk to take."

"Then the word 'attorney'!"

"Might have sounded like 'Tierney,'" Ellery said, "because of the same difficulty with his *r*'s." He shook his head. "An extraordinary situation that wouldn't occur once in a million cases. But it did in this one."

"Wait—a—minute," the Inspector articulated. "Hold your horses, Professor! There's one thing Benedict could have said that you wouldn't—you couldn't—have misunderstood. Same as if he'd put his finger on Marsh in front of witnesses! Marsh was the only *man* besides himself in the house—all the rest were women. Why didn't Benedict simply say the word 'man' and take the chance you'd understand he meant Marsh?"

"Just what I asked myself, dad. But he didn't, and naturally I wondered why. Of course, he might not have thought of it. But suppose he had? The possibility raised a fascinating line of speculation. If he thought of saying 'man' and rejected it in those endless few seconds, then—as in the case of the names—there must have been a basis for similar confusion—"

"But no name in the case sounded like 'man,'" the Inspector objected.

"Yes, but did we know all the names in the case? We did not. There was one conspicuous omission. We didn't know Laura's last name! That's what suggested to me that Laura's surname might be M-a-n-n or might begin with M-a-n or M-a-double n—Manners, Mannheimer, something like that. It turned out to be Manzoni. That must have been, then, why Johnny didn't say it. He was afraid that, if he could get out only the first syllable be-

fore he died or became unconscious, we'd believe—
when we discovered Laura's family name—that he'd
been accusing her of killing him."

The old man was shaking his head. "I never heard
anything like this in my whole life! But Ellery, you said
Benedict did identify his killer to you. The old dying-
message thing you're so crazy about."

"Could it be premature senility?" Ellery made a face.
"At the time I didn't even realize it was a dying message! And then I dismissed it from my alleged mind.
Dad, what was it Johnny said to me over the phone
when I asked him who had attacked him?"

"He said some stupid thing like he was home, or something like that."

"It wasn't stupid, and he didn't say *he was* home.
He uttered the one word, 'home.' In fact, he repeated
it three times. I thought he meant he was calling from
home, that is, from the main house, in his muddled
dying condition answering a 'who' question with a
'where' answer. I should have taken into account at
least the possibility that when I asked 'Who' he'd answered 'who'."

"Who—'Home'? 'Home' isn't a who, Ellery. Unless it
was somebody's name. But there wasn't anybody
named—" The Inspector looked startled. "He didn't
finish," he said slowly. "It was a longer word—*beginning* with 'home'."

"Yes," Ellery said, muffled, out of a well of self-
disgust. "If Johnny had finished the word, or I'd had
the mother wit I was presumably born with—we'd have
solved the mystery of this case actually before the victim drew his last breath."

"Then, Ellery, what Benedict meant to say was the
word—"

"Homosexual."

About the Author

Ellery Queen is a collaboration of Frederic Dannay and Manfred B. Lee, whose total sales in various editions published throughout the world are estimated at more than 100,000,000 copies. Ellery Queen popularized the dramatic mystery on radio, in a program called *The Adventures of Ellery Queen,* which was on the air weekly for nine years, and in 1950 *TV Guide* awarded the Ellery Queen program its national award for the best mystery show on TV. Ellery Queen has won five annual Edgars (the national Mystery Writers of America awards, similar to the Oscars of Hollywood), including the Grand Master award of 1960, and both the silver and gold Gertrudes awarded by Pocket Books, Inc.

Anthony Boucher described Queen best when he said, "Ellery Queen *is* the American detective story."